D1246362

destined

(book # 4 in the vampire journals)

Morgan Rice

Books by Morgan Rice

THE SORCERER'S RING
A QUEST OF HEROES
A MARCH OF KINGS
A FEAST OF DRAGONS
A CLASH OF HONOR
A VOW OF GLORY
A CHARGE OF VALOR
A RITE OF SWORDS

THE SURVIVAL TRILOGY
ARENA ONE (BOOK #1)
ARENA TWO (BOOK #2)

the Vampire Legacy
resurrected (book #1)
craved (book #2)

the Vampire Journals
turned (book #1)
loved (book #2)
betrayed (book #3)
destined (book #4)
desired (book #5)
betrothed (book #6)
vowed (book #7)
found (book #8)

FACT:

In 2009, the first intact corpse of a supposed vampire was discovered, on the small island of Lazzaretto Nuovo, in the Venice lagoon. The vampire, a woman who died by plague in the 16th century, was found buried with a brick in her mouth—supporting the medieval belief that vampires were behind plagues like the Black Death.

FACT:

Venice in the 1700s was unlike any place on earth. People flocked there from around the world to join in its lavish parties and balls, and to dress in elaborate costumes and masks. It was normal for people to walk the streets in full costume. For the first time in history, there was no longer gender inequality. Women, previously kept down by authority, could now disguise themselves as men, and could thus gain access to anywhere they wished....

"O my love! my wife!
Death, that hath suck'd the honey of thy breath,
Hath had no power yet upon thy beauty:
Thou art not conquer'd; beauty's ensign yet
Is crimson in thy lips and in thy cheeks…"

--William Shakespeare, *Romeo and Juliet*

CHAPTER ONE

Assisi, Umbria (Italy)
(1790)

Caitlin Paine awoke slowly, completely enveloped in the blackness. She tried to open her eyes, to get her bearings on where she was, but it didn't do any good. She went to move her hands, her arms—but that didn't work, either. She felt covered, immersed in a soft texture, and she couldn't figure out what it was. It was heavy, weighing her down, and with each passing moment, it seemed to get heavier.

She tried to breathe, but as she did, she realized her passageways were blocked.

Panicking, Caitlin tried to take a deep breath through her mouth, but when she did, she felt something get lodged deep in her throat. Its smell filled her nose, and she finally realized what it was: soil. She was immersed in soil, covering her face and eyes and nose, entering her mouth. She realized it was heavy because it was weighing down on her, getting heavier by the second, suffocating her.

Unable to breathe, unable to see, Caitlin entered into full-fledged panic. She tried to move her legs, her arms, but they, too, were weighed down. In a fit, she struggled for all she was worth, and finally managed to dislodge her arms just a bit; she eventually raised them up, higher and higher. Finally, she broke through the soil, and felt her hands make contact with the air. With a renewed strength, she flailed with all she had, frantically scraping and clawing the soil off of her.

Caitlin finally managed to sit up, soil pouring all over her. She brushed at the dirt clinging to her face, her eyelashes, pulled it out of her mouth, her nose. She used both hands, hysterical, and finally, cleared enough to be able to breathe.

Hyperventilating, she took in huge, gulping breaths, never more grateful to be able to breathe. As she caught her breath, she began coughing, wracking her lungs, spitting out soil from her mouth and nose.

Caitlin pried open her eyes, eyelashes still caked together, and managed to open them enough to see where she was. It was sunset. The countryside. She was lying immersed in a mound of soil, in a small, rural cemetery. As she looked out, she saw the stunned faces of a dozen humble villagers, dressed in rags, staring down at her in utter shock. Beside her was a gravedigger, a beefy man, distracted by his shoveling. He still didn't notice, didn't even look her way as he reached over, shoveled another pile of dirt, and threw it her way.

Before Caitlin could react, the new shovelful of dirt hit her right in the face, covering her eyes and nose again. She swatted it away, and sat up straighter, wiggling her legs, using all her effort to get out from under the fresh, heavy soil.

The gravedigger finally noticed. As he went to throw another shovelful, he saw her, and jumped back. The shovel dropped slowly from his hands, and he took several steps back.

A scream punctured the silence. It came from one of the villagers, the shrill shriek of an old, superstitious woman, who stared down at what should have been the fresh corpse of Caitlin, now rising from the earth. She screamed and screamed.

The other villagers were divided in their reactions. A few of them turned and fled, sprinting to get away. Others simply covered their mouths with their hands, too speechless to say a word. But a few of the men, holding torches, seem to vacillate between fear and anger. They took a few tentative steps towards Caitlin, and she could see from their expressions, and from their raised farm instruments, that they were getting ready to attack.

Where am I? she desperately wondered. *Who are these people?*

As disoriented as she was, Caitlin still had the presence of mind to realize she had to act quickly.

She scraped away at the mound of soil keeping her legs pinned down, clawing at it furiously. But the soil was wet and heavy, and it was slow going. It made her remember a time with her brother Sam, on a beach somewhere, when he had buried her up to her head. She hadn't been able to move. She had begged him to free her, and he had made her wait for hours.

She felt so helpless, so trapped, that, despite herself, she began to cry. She wondered where her vampire strength had gone. Was she merely human again? It felt that way. Mortal. Weak. Just like everybody else.

She suddenly felt scared. Very, very scared.

"Somebody, please, help me!" Caitlin called out, trying to lock eyes with any of the women in the crowd, hoping for a sympathetic face.

But there were none. Instead, there were just looks of shock and fear.

And anger. A mob of men, farm instruments held high, was creeping towards her. She didn't have much time.

She tried to appeal directly to them.

"Please!" Caitlin cried, "it's not what you think! I mean you no harm. Please, don't hurt me! Help me get out of here!"

But that only seemed to embolden them.

"Kill the vampire!" a villager yelled from the crowd. "Kill her again!"

The cry was met by an enthusiastic roar. This mob wanted her dead.

One of the villagers, less afraid than the others, a big brute of a man, came within feet of her. He looked down at her in a callous rage, then raised his pick-axe high. Caitlin could see he was aiming right for her face.

"You will die *this* time!" he yelled, as he wound up.

Caitlin closed her eyes, and from somewhere, deep inside of her, she summoned the rage. It was a primal rage, from some part of her that still existed, and she felt it rising through her toes, coursing through her body, up through her torso. She burned with heat. *It just wasn't fair*, her dying like this, her being attacked, her being so helpless. She hadn't done anything to them. *It just wasn't fair* echoed through her mind again and again, as her rage built to a fever pitch.

The villager swung hard, aiming right for Caitlin's face, and she suddenly felt the burst of strength she needed. In one move, she jumped up out of the soil and onto her feet, and she caught the axe by its wooden handle, mid-swing.

Caitlin could hear a horrified gasp from the mob—startled, they stepped back several feet. Still holding the axe handle, she looked over to see the brute's expression had changed to one of utter fear. Before he could react, she yanked the axe from his hand, leaned back, and kicked him hard in the chest. He went flying back, through the air, a good twenty feet, and he landed into the crowd of villagers, knocking several over with him.

Caitlin raised the axe high, took several quick steps towards them, and with the fiercest expression she could muster, snarled.

The villagers, terrified, raised their hands to their faces, and shrieked. Some took off for the woods, and the ones that remained cowered.

It was the effect Caitlin wanted. She'd scared them just enough to stun them. She dropped the axe and ran right past them, racing through the field, and into the sunset.

As she ran, she was waiting, hoping, for her vampire powers to come back, for her wings to sprout, for her to be able to simply lift off, and fly far away from here.

But she wasn't so lucky. For whatever reason, it wasn't happening.

Have I lost it? she wondered. *Am I merely human again?*

She ran with the speed of a mere, regular human, and felt nothing in her back, no wings, no matter how much she willed it. Was she now just as weak and defenseless as all the others?

Before she could find out the answer, she heard a din rising behind her. She looked over her shoulder and saw the mob of villagers; they were chasing after her. They were screaming, carrying torches, farm instruments, clubs and picking up stones, as they chased her down.

Please God, she prayed. *Let this nightmare end. Just long enough for me to figure out where I am. To become strong again.*

Caitlin looked down and noticed what she was wearing for the first time. It was a long, elaborate black dress, beautifully embroidered, and it went from her neck down to her toes. It was fit for a formal occasion—like a funeral—but certainly not for sprinting. Her legs were restricted by it. She reached down and tore it above the knee. That helped, and she ran faster.

But it still wasn't fast enough. She felt herself getting tired quickly, and the mob behind her seemed to have endless energy. They were closing in fast.

She suddenly felt something sharp on the back of her head, and she reeled from the pain. She stumbled as it hit her, and reached up and touched the spot with her hand. Her hand was covered in blood. She had been hit by a stone.

She saw several stones fly by her, turned, and saw they were throwing stones her way. Another one, painfully, hit her on the small of her back. The mob was now only 20 feet away.

In the distance she saw a steep hill, and at its top, a huge, medieval church and cloister. She ran for it. She hoped that if she could just make it there, perhaps she could find refuge from these people.

But as she was hit again, on the shoulder, by another rock, she realized it would do no good. The church was too far, she was losing steam, and the mob was getting too close. She had no choice but to turn and fight. Ironic, she thought. After all she'd been through, after all the vampire battles, after even surviving a trip back in time, she might end up dead by a stupid mob of villagers.

Caitlin stopped in her tracks, turned and faced the mob. If she was going to die, at least she'd go down fighting.

As she stood there, she closed her eyes and breathed. She focused, and the world around her stopped. She felt her bare feet in the grass, rooted to the earth, and slowly but surely felt a primal strength rise up and wash over her. She willed herself to remember; to remember the rage; to remember her innate, primal strength. At one time she had trained and fought with a superhuman strength. She *willed* for it to come back. She felt that somewhere, somehow, it still lurked deep inside of her.

As she stood there, she thought of all the mobs in her life, all the bullies, all the jerks. She thought of her mother, who begrudged her even the smallest kindness; remembered the bullies who'd chased her and Jonah down that alleyway New York. She thought of those bullies in that barn in the Hudson Valley, Sam's friends. And she remembered Cain's introduction on Pollepel. It seemed that there were always bullies, bullies everywhere. Running from them had never done her any good. Like she'd always done, she'd just have to stand and fight.

As she dwelled on the injustice of it all, the rage built, coursed through her. It doubled and tripled, until she felt her very veins swelling with it, felt her muscles about to burst.

At just that moment, the mob closed in. A villager raised his club and swung for her head. With her newfound power, Caitlin ducked just in time, bent down, and threw him over her shoulder. He went flying several feet in the air, and landed on his back in the grass.

Another man reached back with a large stone, getting ready to bring it down on her head; but she reached up and grabbed his wrist and snapped it back. He sank to his knees, screaming.

A third villager swung at her with his hoe, but she was too quick: she spun around and grabbed it mid-swing. She yanked it from his hands, wound up, and cracked him in the head.

The hoe, six feet long, was just what she needed. She swung it in a wide circle, knocking down anyone within range; within moments, she established a large perimeter around her. She saw a villager reach back with a large stone, gearing up to throw it at her, and she hurled the hoe right at him. It hit him in the hand and knocked the stone from it.

Caitlin ran into the dazed crowd, grabbed a torch from the hand of an old woman, and swung it wildly. She managed to light a section of the tall, dry grass on fire, and there were screams, as many villagers rushed back, in fear. When the wall of fire got large enough, she reached back and hurled the torch directly into the mob. It went flying through the air and landed on the back of a man's tunic, lighting him and the person next to him on fire. The mob quickly gathered around them to put it out.

It served Caitlin's purpose. The villagers were finally distracted enough to give her the running room she needed to take off. She wasn't interested in hurting them. She just wanted them to leave her alone. She just needed to catch her breath, to figure out where she was.

She turned and raced back up the hill for the church. She felt a newfound strength and speed, felt herself bounding up the hill, and knew she was outrunning them. She only hoped that the church would be open, and would let her in.

As she ran up the hill, feeling the grass beneath her bare feet, dusk fell, and she saw several torches being lit in the town square, and along the cloister's walls. As she got closer, she spotted a night watchman, high up on a parapet. He looked down at her, and fear crossed his face. He reached a torch above his head, and screamed: "Vampire! Vampire!"

As he did, the church bells rang out.

Caitlin saw torches appear on all sides of her. People were coming out of the woodwork in every direction, as the watchman kept screaming, and as the bells tolled. It was a witch-hunt, and they all seemed to be heading directly for her.

Caitlin increased her speed, running so hard that her ribs hurt. Gasping for breath, she reached the oak doors of the church just in time. She yanked one of them open, then wheeled and slammed it behind her with a bang.

Inside, she looked frantically around, and spotted a shepherd's staff. She grabbed it and slid it across the double doors, barring them.

The second she did, she heard a tremendous crash at the door, as dozens of hands pounded on it. The doors shook, but did not give way. The staff was holding—at least for now.

Caitlin quickly surveyed the room. The church, thankfully, was empty. It was huge, its arched ceilings soaring hundreds of feet high. It was a cold, empty place, hundreds of pews on a marble floor; on the far side, above the altar, hung several burning candles.

As she looked, she could have sworn she saw movement at the far end of the room.

The pounding grew more intense, and the door began to shake. Caitlin burst into action, running down the aisle, towards the altar. As she reached it, she saw she had been right: there was someone there.

Kneeling quietly, with his back to her, was a priest.

Caitlin wondered how he could ignore all this, ignore her presence, how he could be so deeply immersed in prayer in a time like this. She hoped he wouldn't turn her over to her mob.

"Hello?" Caitlin said.

He didn't turn.

Caitlin hurried over to the other side, facing him. He was an older man, with white hair, clean shaven, and light blue eyes that seem to stare into space as he knelt in prayer. He didn't bother looking up at her. There was something else, too, that she sensed about him. Even in her current state, she could tell that there was something different about him. She knew that he was of her kind. A vampire.

The pounding grew louder, and one of the hinges broke, and Caitlin looked back in fear. This mob seemed determined, and she didn't know where else to go.

"Help me, please!" Caitlin urged.

He continued his prayer for several moments. Finally, without looking at her, he said: "How can they kill what's already dead?"

There was a splintering of wood.

"*Please*," she urged. "Don't turn me over to them."

He rose slowly, quiet and composed, and pointed to the altar. "In there," he said. "Behind the curtain. There's a trap door. Go!"

She followed his finger, but saw only a large podium, covered in a satin cloth. She ran over to it, pulled back the cloth, and saw the trap door. She opened it, and squeezed her body into the small space.

Tucked in, she peered out through the tiny crack. She watched the priest hurry over to a side door, and kick it open with surprising force.

Just as he did, the main front doors were kicked in by the mob, and they came tearing down the aisle.

Caitlin quickly slid back the curtain all the way. She hoped they hadn't spotted her. She watched through a crack in the wood, and saw just enough to see the mob racing down the aisle, seemingly right for her.

"That way!" screamed the priest. "The vampire fled that way!"

He pointed out the side door, and the mob rushed right past him, and back into the night.

After several seconds, the never-ending stream of bodies fled from the church, and all was finally silent.

The priest closed the door, locking it behind them.

She could hear his footsteps, walking towards her, and Caitlin, shaking with fear, with cold, slowly opened the trap door.

He slid back the curtain and looked down at her.

He extended a gentle hand.

"Caitlin," he said, and smiled. "We've been waiting a very long time for you."

CHAPTER TWO

Rome, 1790

Kyle stood in the darkness, breathing hard. There were few things he hated more than confined spaces, and as he reached out in the blackness and felt the stone encasing him, he broke into a sweat. Trapped. Nothing was worse for him.

He reached back and with his fist and smashed a hole right through the stone. It shattered into pieces, and he shielded his eyes from the daylight.

If Kyle hated anything more than being trapped, it was being struck head-on by daylight, especially without his skin wraps on. He quickly jumped through the rubble and took shelter behind a wall.

Kyle breathed deep and surveyed his surroundings, disoriented, as he wiped the dust from his eyes. This was what he hated about time travel: he never knew exactly where he'd surface. He hadn't attempted it for centuries, and he wouldn't have now if it weren't for that never-ending thorn in his side, Caitlin.

It hadn't taken long after she'd left New York for Kyle to realize that his war was only partially won. With her still on the loose, with her tracking down the shield, he realized he could never rest at ease. He had been on the brink of winning the war, of enslaving the entire human race, of becoming the unilateral leader of the vampire race himself. But she, this pathetic little girl, was stopping him. As long as the shield was at large, he could not assume absolute power. He had no choice but to track her down and kill her. And if that meant going back in time, then that was what he would do.

Breathing hard, Kyle quickly extracted a skin wrap and wrapped his arms, neck and torso. He looked around, and realized he was in a mausoleum. It looked Roman, from its markings. *Rome.*

He hadn't been here in ages. He had stirred up too much dust by smashing the marble, and the sediment hung thickly in the daylight, making it hard to tell. He took a deep breath, braced himself, and headed outside.

He was right: it was Rome. He looked out, saw the Italian Cypress trees, and knew he could be nowhere else. He realized that he stood at the top of the Roman forum, its green grass, its hills and valleys and crumbling monuments stretched out before him in a gentle slope. It brought back memories. He had killed many people here, back when it was in use, and he had nearly been killed here once himself. He smiled at the thought of it. It was his kind of place.

And it was the perfect place to land. The Pantheon was not far away, and within minutes, he could be before the judges of the Roman Grand Council, its most powerful coven, and have all the answers he needed. He would soon know where Caitlin was, and if all went well, have their permission to kill her.

Not that he needed it. It was just courtesy, vampire etiquette, the following of thousand-year-old tradition. One always sought permission for a kill in someone else's territory.

But if they refused, he would hardly back down. It could make his life difficult, but he would kill anyone who stood in his way.

Kyle breathed deep in the Roman air, and he felt at home. It had been too long since he'd been back. He had gotten too caught up in being in New York, in vampire politics, in a modern time and place. This was more his style. He could see the horses in the distance, the dirt roads, and guessed he was likely in the eighteenth century. Perfect. Rome was urban, but still naïve, still had 200 years of catching up to do.

As Kyle checked himself, he saw he had survived the trip back in time fairly well. In other trips, he had been far more beaten up, had needed more recovery time. But not this time. He felt stronger than he ever had, ready to go. He felt his wings would sprout right away, that he could fly directly to the Pantheon if he wished, and put his plan into action.

But he wasn't quite ready. He hadn't had a vacation in a long time, and it felt good being back. He wanted to explore a bit, to see and remember what it had been like to be here.

Kyle bounded down the hill with his incredible speed, and in no time at all, he was out of the Forum and onto the bustling, crowded streets of Rome.

He marveled that even 200 years earlier, Rome was still crowded as could be.

Kyle slowed his pace as he blended into the crowd, walking alongside them. It was a mass of humanity. The wide boulevard, still made of dirt, held thousands of people, hurrying in every direction. It also held horses of all shapes and sizes, along with horse-drawn carts, wagons and carriages. The streets stank of body odor and horse manure. It was now all coming back to Kyle, the lack of plumbing, the lack of bathing—the stench of old times. It made him sick.

Kyle felt himself being jostled in every direction, as the crowd grew thicker and thicker, people of all races and classes hurrying to and fro. He marveled at the primitive storefronts, selling old-fashioned Italian hats. He marveled at the small boys, dressed in rags, who ran up to him, holding out pieces of fruit to sell. Some things never changed.

Kyle turned down a narrow, seedy alleyway, one he remembered well, hoping that it was still as it once was. He was delighted to find that it was: before him stood dozens of prostitutes, leaning against the walls, calling out to him as he walked.

Kyle smiled wide.

As he approached one of them—a large, buxom woman with dyed, red hair and too much makeup—she reached up and stroked his face with her hand.

"Hey big boy," she said, "looking for a good time? How much do you have?"

Kyle smiled, draped his arm around her, and directed her down a side alleyway.

She gladly followed.

As soon as they turned the corner, she said, "You didn't answer my question. How much do you got—"

It was a question she would never finish.

Before she could finish speaking, Kyle had already sunk his teeth deep into her neck.

She tried to scream, but he clamped her mouth shut with his free hand, and pulled her closer, drinking and drinking. He felt the human blood rush through his veins, and felt exhilarated. He had been parched, dehydrated. The time travel had exhausted him, and this was exactly what he'd needed to restore his spirits.

As he felt her body go limp, he sucked more and more, drinking more than he could possibly need. Finally, feeling completely sated, he let her limp body drop to the floor.

As he turned and prepared to exit, a huge man, unshaven, missing a tooth, approached. He extracted a dagger from his belt.

The man looked down at the dead woman, then up to Kyle, and grimaced.

"That was my property," the man said. "You better got money for that."

The man took two steps towards Kyle, and lunged at him with the dagger.

Kyle, with this lightning fast reflexes, easily sidestepped, grabbed the man's wrist, and pulled it back in one motion, breaking his arm in half.

The man screamed, but before he could finish, Kyle snatched the dagger from his hands and in the same motion, slashed his throat. He let the dead body fall limp to the street.

Kyle looked down at the dagger, an intricate little thing with an ivory handle, and nodded. It wasn't half bad. He tucked into his belt and wiped the blood from his mouth with the back of his hand. He breathed deeply, and, finally content, walked down the alleyway and back onto the street.

Oh, how he had missed Rome.

CHAPTER THREE

Caitlin walked with the priest down the aisle of the church, as he finished barring the front door and sealing off all the other entrances. The sun had set, and he lit torches as he went, gradually lighting its vast rooms.

Caitlin looked up and noticed all of the huge crosses, and wondered why she felt so at peace here. Weren't vampires supposed to be afraid of churches? Of crosses? She remembered the White Coven's home in the New York Cloisters, and the crosses that had lined the walls. Caleb had told her that certain vampire races embraced churches. He had launched into a long monologue about the history of the vampire race and its relationship with Christianity, but she hadn't listened closely at the time, too enamored of him. Now, she wished she'd had.

The vampire priest led Caitlin through a side door, and Caitlin found herself descending a flight of stone steps. They walked down an arched, medieval passageway, and he continued to light torches as he went.

"I don't think they'll be back," he said, locking another entrance as he went. "They'll comb the countryside for you, and when they don't find you, go back to their homes. That's what they always do."

Caitlin felt safe here, and she was so grateful for this man's help. She wondered why he had helped her, why he had put his life on the line for her.

"Because I'm of your kind," he said, turning and looking right at her, his piercing blue eyes boring through her.

Caitlin always forgot how easily vampires could read each other's minds. But for a moment, she had forgotten that he was one of hers.

"Not all of us fear churches," he said, answering her thoughts again. "You know that our race is splintered. Our kind—the benevolent kind—need churches. We thrive in them."

As they turned down another corridor, down another small flight of steps, Caitlin wondered where he was leading them. So many questions raced through her mind, she didn't know what to ask him first.

"Where am I?" she asked, and realized, as she did, that it was the first thing she'd said to him since they'd met. All her questions came pouring out in a rush. "What country am I in? What year is it?"

He smiled as they walked, the age lines bunching up in his face. He was a short, frail man, with white hair, clean-shaven, and a grandfatherly face. He wore the elaborate garments of a priest, and even for a vampire, he looked very old. She wondered how many centuries he'd been on this earth. She felt kindness and warmth radiate from him, and felt very at peace around him.

"So many questions," he finally said, with a smile. "I understand. It is a lot for you. Well, to begin with, you are in Umbria. In the small town of Assisi."

She wracked her brain, trying to figure out where that was.

"Italy?" she asked.

"In the future, yes, this region will be a part of a country called Italy," he said, "but not now. We are still independent. Remember," he smiled, "you are no longer in the 21st century— as you may have guessed from the dress and behavior of those villagers."

"What year is it?" Caitlin asked quietly, almost afraid to know the answer. Her heart beat faster.

"You are in the 18th century," he answered. "To be more precise: the year 1790."

1790. Assisi. Umbria. Italy.

The thought of it overwhelmed her. It all felt surreal, as if she were in a dream. She could hardly believe this was really happening, that she was really, actually, *here*, in this time and place. That time travel really worked.

She also felt a bit relieved: of all the times and places she could have landed, Italy in 1790 didn't sound too foreboding. It wasn't like landing in prehistoric times.

"Why were those people trying to kill me? And who are you?"

"Despite all of our advances, this is still a somewhat primitive and superstitious time," he said. "Even in this age of luxury and decadence, alas, there are still scores of commoners who live very much in fear of us.

"You see, the small mountain village of Assisi has always been a stronghold for our kind. It is frequented by vampires, and always has been. Our kind of vampire only feed on their livestock. Still, over time, the villagers begin to take notice.

"Sometimes they'll spot one of us. And when they do, the situation becomes intolerable. So every now and again, we let them bury us. We let them go through their silly little human rituals, let them feel as if they've gotten rid of us. And when they're not looking, we simply rise again and return back to our lives.

"But sometimes, a vampire rises back too soon, or is seen rising back, and then there comes the mob. It will blow over. These things always do. It brings unwanted attention to our kind, but only temporarily."

"I'm sorry," Caitlin said, feeling badly.

"Don't worry," he said, "This was your first time travel. You couldn't control it. It takes some getting used to. Even the best of us can't control re-surfacing very well. It's always hard to say exactly when or where we'll end up. You did fine," he said, gently placing a hand on her wrist.

They walked down another corridor, this one with low, vaulted ceilings.

"Besides, you didn't do all that bad," he added. "After all, you knew enough to come here."

Caitlin remembered spotting the church as she'd sprinted through the field.

"But it just seemed like the logical place to go," she answered. "It was the first building I saw, and it seemed like a fortress."

He smiled, shaking his head. "There is no such thing as coincidence in the vampire world," he said. "Everything is destined. A building that seems secure to you might seem frail to someone else. No, you chose this spot for a reason. A very specific reason. And you were led to me."

"But you're a priest."

He shook his head slightly. "You're still very young, and you still have a lot to learn. We have our own religion, our own creed. It is not very different from that of the church. One can be a vampire and still involved in religious life. Especially our type of vampire," he said. "I even help the humans in their daily spiritual life. After all, I have the benefit and wisdom of thousands of years on this planet—unlike human priests. Luckily, the humans don't know I am not of their kind. For all they know, I am the town priest, and always have been."

Caitlin's mind spun, as she tried to reconcile it all. The image of a vampire priest seemed so paradoxical to her. The notion of a vampire religion, of its working within the church…it all seemed so strange.

As fascinating as all of this was, what she really wanted to know was not about vampires, or churches, or religion. She wanted to know about Caleb. Had he survived the trip? Was he alive? Where was he?

And she wanted desperately to know about their child. Was she still pregnant? Had the baby survived?

She thought these questions very strongly, and hoped the priest would pick them up, and answer her back.

But he didn't.

She knew he'd heard her thoughts, and was choosing not to respond. He was forcing her to ask these questions aloud. And, as he probably knew, they were questions she was afraid to ask.

"And what of Caleb?" she finally asked, her voice shaking. She was too nervous to ask about her child.

She looked over at him and saw his smile fade, as the slightest wince crossed his face.

Her heart dropped.

Please, she thought. *Please don't tell me bad news.*

"Some things you're going to have to find out for yourself," he said slowly. "Some things I am not meant to tell you. It is a journey you must take. You and you alone."

"But is he here?" she asked hopefully. "Did he make it?"

The priest, walking alongside her, tightened his lips. He let her questions hang in the air, unanswered, for what felt like forever.

Finally, they stopped before another flight of steps, and he turned and looked at her. "I wish I could tell you more," he said. "I really do."

He turned, raised his torch, and led the way down another small flight of steps.

They entered a long, vaulted corridor, all the ceilings here gilded and intricately designed. They were entirely covered with frescoes, brightly designed, and in between them were arches, lined with gold. The ceiling shone.

So did the floor. It was a beautiful, pink marble, and looked freshly cleaned. This subterranean level of the church was gorgeous, looked like an ancient treasure chamber.

"Wow," Caitlin heard herself say out loud. "What is this place?"

"It is a place of miracles. You are in the church of Saint Francis of Assisi. This is also his resting place. It is a very holy place in our religion. People—humans and vampires alike— pilgrimage here, from thousands of miles away, just to be in this spot. Francis was the saint of animals, and he was also the saint of all living creatures outside of the human race—including our kind. It is said that miracles happen here. We are protected here by his energy.

"You did not land here by accident," he continued. "This place is a portal for you. It is a launching pad for you to begin your journey, *your* pilgrimage."

He turned and faced her.

"What you still fail to see," he said, "is that you are on a journey. And some pilgrimages take years, and many, many miles."

Caitlin thought. It was all overwhelming to her. She did not want to be on a journey. She wanted to be back home, with Caleb, safe and secure, in the 21st century, this whole nightmare behind her. She was tired of traveling, of always being on the run, of always searching. She just wanted a normal life again, the life of a teenage girl.

But she stopped herself from that way of thinking. It wasn't helpful, she knew. Things had changed—permanently—and they would never be the same again. She reminded herself that change was the new normal. She was no longer the same old, average, human Caitlin. She was older now. Wiser. And whether she liked it or not, she was on a special mission. She just had to accept it.

"But what is my pilgrimage?" Caitlin asked. "What is my destination? Where is it exactly that I'm going?"

He led her to the end of the final corridor, and they stopped before a large, elaborate tomb.

Caitlin could feel the energy coming off of the tomb, and she knew right away that this was the tomb of Saint Francis. She felt recharged just standing near it, felt herself growing stronger, coming back into her own. She wondered again if she had come back as a human or as a vampire. She missed her powers dearly.

"Yes, you are still a vampire," he said. "Do not worry. It is just taking time for you to come back to your own."

She was embarrassed that she forgot, again, to guard her thoughts, but she felt comforted by his words.

"You are a very special person, Caitlin," he said. "You are very much needed to our race. Without you, I would even go so far as to say, our entire race, and the entire human race, will be on the brink of extinction. We need you. We need your help."

"But what am I supposed to?" she asked.

"We need you to find the Shield," he said. "And in order to find the Shield, you will need to find your father. He, and only he, holds it. And in order to find him, you will need to find your coven. Your *true* coven."

"But I have no idea where to begin," she said. "I don't even know why I'm in this place and time. Why Italy? Why 1790?"

"The answers to these questions you are going to have to find out for yourself. But I assure you you have very special reasons for being back in this lifetime. Special people to see, actions to fulfill. And that this place and time will lead you to the Shield."

Caitlin thought.

"But I have no idea where my father is. I have no idea where to begin."

He turned to her and smiled. "But you do," he answered. "That is your problem. You don't trust your intuition. You need to learn to search deep within yourself. Try it now. Close your eyes, breathe deeply."

Caitlin did as he said.

"Ask yourself: where do I need to go next?"

Caitlin did so, wracking her brain. Nothing happened.

"Listen to the sound of your breathing. Let your mind still."

As Caitlin did so, as she really focused and relaxed, images began to flash in her mind. She finally opened her eyes and looked at him.

"I see two places," she said. "Florence, and Venice."

"Yes," he said. "Very good."

"But I'm confused. Where do I go?"

"There are no wrong choices in a journey. Each path just brings us to a different place.

The choice is yours. You have a very strong destiny, but you also have free will. You can choose at any step. Now, for example, you are faced with a pivotal choice. In Florence, you will fulfill your obligations, come closer to the Shield. It is what is needed of you. But in Venice, you will fulfill matters of the heart. You will have to choose between your mission and your heart."

Caitlin's heart soared.

Matters of the heart. Did that mean that Caleb was in Venice?

She felt her heart drawn to Venice. Yet, intellectually, she knew that Florence was where she *should* be in order to do what was expected of her.

She felt torn already.

"You are a grown woman now," he said. "The choice is yours to make. But if you follow your heart, there will be heartbreak," he warned. "The road of the heart is never easy. And never expected."

"I feel so confused," she said.

"We do our best work in dreams," he said. "There is a cloisters next door, and you can sleep here for the night, rest, and decide in the morning. By then, you'll be fully recovered."

"Thank you," she said, reaching out and taking his hand.

He turned to go, and as he did, her heart pounded. There was one more question she needed to ask him, the most important one of all. But a part of her was too scared to ask it. She was trembling. She opened her mouth to speak, but it turned dry.

He was walking down the corridor, about to turn away, when finally, she mustered the courage.

"Wait!" she yelled. Then softer, "Please, I have one more question."

He stopped in his tracks, but kept his back to her. Oddly enough, he did not turn back around, as if he sensed what she was about to ask.

"My baby," she said, in a soft, trembling voice. "Is he…she…did it make it? The trip? Am I still pregnant?"

He slowly turned, faced her. Then he lowered his eyes.

"I'm sorry," he finally said, so soft that she wasn't sure if she heard it. "You've come back in time. Children can only move forward. Your child lives, but not in this time. Only in the future."

"But…" she began, trembling, "I thought vampires can only travel back in time, not forwards."

"True," he said. "I am afraid that your child lives in a time and place without you." He lowered his eyes again. "I am so sorry," he added.

With those final words, he turned and left.

And Caitlin felt as if a dagger had been plunged into her heart.

CHAPTER FOUR

Caitlin sat in the stark room of the Franciscan monastery and looked out through the open window, into the night. She had finally stopped crying. It had been hours since she'd left the priest, since she'd heard the news of her lost child. She hadn't been able to stop the tears, or to stop thinking about the life she would have led. It was all too painful.

But after many hours, she cried herself out, and now all that was left were dried up tears on her cheeks. She looked out the window, trying to distract herself, and breathed deep.

The Umbrian countryside spread out before her, and from this vantage point, high up on a hill, she could the rolling hills of Assisi. There was a full moon out, enough light for her to see that this was a truly beautiful countryside. She saw the small, country cottages dotting the landscape, the smoke rising from the chimneys, and she could already feel that this was a quieter, more relaxed time in history.

Caitlin turned and surveyed her small room, lit only by the moonlight and a small candle burning on a wall sconce. It was made entirely of stone, with only a simple bed in the corner. She marveled at how it seemed to be her fate to always end up in a cloister. This place couldn't be more different than Pollepel, yet at the same time, the small, medieval room reminded her of the room she'd had there. It was designed for introspection.

Caitlin examined the smooth, stone floor, and saw, near the window, two slight imprints, a few inches apart, in the shape of a knee. She wondered how many nuns had prayed here, had knelt before the window. This room had probably seen hundreds of years of use.

Caitlin went over to the small bed, and laid down. It was just a stone slab, really, with the tiniest bit of straw. She tried to get comfortable, rolling on her side—and then she felt something. She reached over and extracted it, and realized with delight what it was: her journal.

She held it up, so happy to have it by her side. Her old trusted friend, it seemed to be the one thing that had survived the journey back. Holding it, this real, tangible thing, made her realize that this was not all a dream. She was really here. Everything had really happened.

A modern pen slipped out of its pages and landed on her lap. She held it up and examined it, thinking.

Yes, she decided. That was exactly what she needed to do. To write. To process. Everything had happened so fast, she'd hardly had time to catch her breath. She needed to play it through in her mind, to think back, to remember. How had she gotten here? What had happened? Where was she going?

She wasn't sure if she knew the answers herself anymore. But by writing, she hoped she could remember.

Caitlin turned the brittle pages over until she found an empty page. She sat up and leaned against the wall, curled her knees to her chest and began to write.

*

How did I end up here? In Assisi? In Italy? In 1790? On the one hand, it doesn't seem like long ago that I was back in the 21st century, in New York, living a normal teenage life. On the other hand, it seems like forever….How did it all begin?

I remember, first, the hunger pangs. My not understanding what they were. Jonah. Carnegie Hall.

My first feeding. My inexplicably turning into a vampire. A half-breed is what they called me. I'd felt like I'd wanted to die. All I'd ever wanted was to be like everybody else.

Then there was Caleb. His saving me from the evil coven, rescuing me. His coven in the Cloisters. But they cast me out, as human and vampire relationships were forbidden. I was on my own again—that is, until Caleb rescued me again.

My quest for my father, for the mythical sword that could spare the human race from a vampire war, led Caleb and I all over the place, from one historic place to another. We found the sword, and it got taken from us. As always, Kyle was waiting to ruin things.

But not before I had time to realize what I was becoming. And not before Caleb and I had time to find each other. After they stole the sword, after they stabbed me, as I was dying, he turned me, and saved me once again.

But it didn't turn out like I'd thought. I saw Caleb with his ex-wife, Sera, and I imagined the worst. I was wrong, but it was too late. He fled, far from me, and into danger. On Pollepel island, I recovered, and trained, and made friends—vampires—closer than I'd ever had. Especially Polly. And Blake—so mysterious, so beautiful. He almost stole my heart. But I came to my senses just in time. I learned I was pregnant, and I realized I had to find and save Caleb from the vampire war.

I went to save Caleb, but it was too late. My own brother Sam, deceived us. He betrayed me, made me think he was someone else. It was because of him that I thought Caleb was not really Caleb, and I killed him, my love. With the sword. With my own hands. I still can't forgive myself.

But I brought Caleb back to Pollepel. I tried to revive him, to bring him back, if there was any possible way. I'd told Aiden that I would do anything, sacrifice anything. I asked him if he could send us back in time.

Aiden had warned me that it might not work. And that if it did, we might not be together. But I'd insisted. I had to.

And now, here I am. Alone. In a foreign place and time. My child gone. And maybe even Caleb gone, too.

Did I make a mistake to come back?

I know I need to find my father, to find the shield. But without Caleb by my side, I don't know if I'll have the strength to go on.

I feel so confused. I don't know what to do next.

Please, God, help me....

*

As the sun rose in a huge ball over the horizon, Caitlin ran through the streets of New York. It was the apocalypse. Cars were turned over, bodies lay about, and there was devastation everywhere. She ran and ran, down avenues which never seemed to end.

As she ran, the world seemed to turn on its axis; as it did, the buildings seemed to disappear. The landscape changed, with the avenues turning into dirt paths, the concrete turning into rolling hills. She felt herself running back in time, from a modern age to another century. She felt that if she just ran faster, she could find her father, her true father, somewhere on the horizon.

She ran through small country villages, and then these, too, faded away.

Soon all that was left was a field of white flowers. As she ran through them, she was delighted to see that he was there, on the horizon, waiting. Her father.

As always, he was silhouetted against the sun, but this time, he felt closer than usual. This time, she could see his face, his expression. He was smiling, waiting for her, arms extended for a hug.

She reached him. She embraced him, and he hugged her tight, his muscled torso holding her.

"Caitlin," he said, his voice exuding such love. "Do you know how close you are? Do you know how much I love you?"

Before she could respond, she spotted something to the side, and saw that, standing on the other side of the field, was Caleb. He held out a hand towards her.

She took several steps towards him, then stopped and faced her father.

He, too, held out a hand.

"Find me in Florence," her father said.

She turned to Caleb.

"Find me in Venice," Caleb said.

She looked back and forth between the two, torn over which way to go.

*

Caitlin woke with a jolt, and sat upright in bed.

She looked around her small room, disoriented.

Finally, she realized it was a dream.

The sun was rising, and she went over to the window, and looked. Assisi in the early morning light was so still, so beautiful. Everyone was still indoors, and smoke rose from the occasional chimney. An early morning mist hung over the fields like a cloud, refracting the light.

Caitlin suddenly wheeled as she heard a creaking noise, and braced herself as she saw her door starting to pry open. She bunched her fists, preparing herself for an unwanted visitor.

But as the door opened wider, she looked down, and her eyes opened wide in delight.

It was Rose, pushing the door open with her nose.

"Rose!" she screamed.

Rose pushed the door open all the way, ran in and leapt up into Caitlin's arms. She licked her face all over, as Caitlin cried in joy.

Caitlin pulled her back and looked her over. She had filled out, grown bigger.

"How did you find me?" Caitlin asked.

Rose licked her back, whining.

Caitlin sat on the edge of the bed, petting her, and thought hard, trying to clear her mind. If Rose had made it back, perhaps Caleb had, too. She felt encouraged.

Intellectually, she knew she needed to go to Florence. To continue the search. She knew that the key to finding her father, the shield, lay there.

But her heart pulled her to Venice.

If there was even a remote chance that Caleb could be there, she had to find out. She just had to.

She decided. She picked up Rose tightly in her arms, took a running start, and leapt out the window.

She knew that she was recovered now, that her wings would sprout.

Sure enough, they did.

And in moments, Caitlin was flying through the early morning air, over the hills of Umbria, and heading north, on the way to Venice.

CHAPTER FIVE

Kyle walked down the narrow streets of the ancient district of Rome. All around him people were closing shops, retiring for the day. Sunset had always been his favorite time of day, the time he began to feel the strongest. He felt his blood pulsing quicker, felt himself growing stronger with each step. He was so happy to be back in the crowded streets of Rome, especially in this century. These pathetic humans were still hundreds of years away from any type of technology, any type of surveillance. He could tear this place apart with a relaxed and easy heart, and not have to worry about being detected.

Kyle turned down Via Del Seminario, and within moments, it opened up, and he found himself in a large, ancient square, The Piazza Della Rotonda.

And there it stood. Kyle stood there, closed his eyes, and breathed deeply. It felt so good to be back. Directly across from him was a place he'd called home for centuries, one of the most important vampire headquarters in the world: the Pantheon.

The Pantheon stood, Kyle was happy to see, as it always had, a massive, ancient stone building, the rear of it jutting out in a circular shape, and its front heralded by huge, imposing stone columns. By day, it was still open to tourists, even during this century. It hosted unseemly mobs of human beings.

But at night, after they closed the doors to the public, the real owners, the *real* occupants of this building, came out in force: the Grand Vampire Council.

Vampires from covens large and small, from all corners of the world, flocked to it, to attend every session every, all night long. The council ruled in all matters, gave permission, or took it away. Nothing happened in the vampire world without their knowing about it, and in most cases, without their approving.

It all fit so perfectly. This building had originally been built as a temple to the pagan gods. It had always been a place of worship, of gathering, for the dark vampire forces. For anyone with eyes to see, it was obvious: there were odes to pagan gods, frescoes, paintings, statues everywhere. Any human sightseer who took the time to read the mission of this place, could only realize what its true purpose was.

And if that were not enough, there were also all the great vampires buried there. It was a living mausoleum, the perfect place for Kyle and his kind to call home.

As Kyle ascended the steps, it felt like a homecoming. He walked right up to the enormous iron double front doors, slammed the metal knocker four times—the vampire signal—and waited.

Moments later, the heavy doors slid open just a few inches, and Kyle saw an unfamiliar face. The door opened wider, just enough to let Kyle in, and then was slammed quickly behind him.

The massive guard, even larger than Kyle, looked down.

"They are expecting you?" he asked warily.

"No."

Kyle, ignoring the guard, took several steps towards the chamber, when suddenly, he felt a cold, icy grip on his arm and stopped. Kyle fumed, burning with rage.

The vampire guard stared down at him with equal rage.

"No one enters without an appointment," he snapped. "You're going to have to leave and come back another time."

"I enter anywhere I choose," Kyle seethed back. "And if you don't remove your hand from my wrist, you're going to suffer greatly."

The guard stared back, and they were in a deadlock.

"I see that some things never change," came a voice. "It's okay, you can let him go."

Kyle felt the grip release, and turned and saw a familiar face: it was Lore, one of the chief advisers to the Council. He stood there, staring at Kyle, smiling, slowly shaking his head.

"Kyle," he said, "I never thought I'd see you again."

Kyle, still fuming from the guard, straightened his jacket and slowly nodded. "I have business with the Council," he said. "It can't wait."

"I'm sorry, old friend," Lore continued, "it's a full agenda for today. Some of them have been waiting for months. Pressing vampire business in every corner of the world, it seems. But if you come back next week, I think I might be able to accommodate—"

Kyle stepped forward. "You don't understand," he said tensely, "I didn't come from this time. I came from the future. Two hundred years into the future. From a vastly different world. The final judgment has arrived. We are on the brink of victory—total victory.

And if I don't see them right away, there will be grave consequences for us all."

As Lore stared back, his smile dropped, as he realized the seriousness; finally, after several tense moments, he cleared his throat. "Follow me."

He turned and strode off, and Kyle followed closely on his heels.

Kyle passed down a long, wide corridor, and within moments, he entered the huge, open chamber. It was immense, wide open, with a soaring, circular ceiling and a marble, shining floor. The room was shaped in a circle, and its periphery was filled with ornate columns and statues looking down on the room, mounted on pedestals.

Standing along the periphery of the room were hundreds of vampires, of every possible race and creed. Kyle knew that these were mostly mercenaries, all as evil as he. They all watched patiently as the Grand Council, on the far side of the room, sat behind their bench and doled out judgment. He felt the electricity in the room.

Kyle walked in, taking it all in. Going to the Council was the right thing to do. He could have tried to ignore them, could have just hunted Caitlin down on his own, but the Council would have intelligence, be able to guide him to her more quickly. More importantly, he needed their official sanction. Finding Caitlin was not just a personal matter, but a matter of the utmost importance to the vampire race. If the Council endorsed him, and he felt sure that they would, he would not only have their sanction, but their resources. He could kill her quicker, and be home faster, ready to finish out his war.

Without their sanction, he would be just another rogue, mercenary vampire. Kyle had no issue with that, but he didn't want to spend his time watching his back: if he acted without their sanction, they might send vampires out to kill him. He felt confident he could handle himself, but he didn't want to have to waste his time and energy that way.

But if they rejected his demands, he was fully prepared to do whatever he had to to hunt her down.

It was ultimately just one more formality in an endless stream of vampire formalities. This etiquette was the glue that held them all together—but it also annoyed him to no end.

As Kyle walked deeper into the chamber, he looked at the Council. They were just as he remembered them. On the far side of the chamber, the 12 judges of the grand Council sat on a raised dais. They were dressed in stark, black robes, all wearing black hoods which covered their faces. Kyle nonetheless knew what these men were. He had faced them many times over the centuries. Once, and only once, had they pulled back their hoods, and had he actually seen their grotesque, aged faces, faces that had walked the planet for millions of years. He flinched at the memory. They were hideous creatures of the night.

Yet they were the Grand Council of his time, and they had always resided here, ever since the Pantheon was built. It was really a part of them, this building, and no one of his kind, not even Kyle, dared cross their judgment. Their powers were just too intense, and the resources at their fingertips too vast. Kyle could maybe get away with killing one or two of them, but the armies they could summon, from every corner of the world, would eventually hunt him down.

The hundreds of vampires in the room came to witness the Council's judgments, and to await their audience. They always lined up neatly along the sides, stood at attention, in a huge circle, on the outskirts, leaving the center of the room entirely open. Save for one person. That was always the person who needed to stand before them in judgment.

Right now, it was some poor soul, standing by himself, trembling in fear as he stood across from them, staring at their inscrutable hoods, waiting for their judgment. Kyle had been in that spot before. It was not pleasant. If they did not like the matter with which you approached them, they might, on a whim, kill you on the spot. You never went before them lightly—it was always a matter of life and death.

"Wait here," Lore whispered to Kyle, as he headed off into the crowd. Kyle stood on the periphery, watching.

As Kyle watched, a judge nodded, ever so slightly, and two vampire soldiers appeared from either side. Each grabbed one arm of the person facing the Council.

"No! NO!" he screamed.

But it didn't do him any good. They dragged him away, as he screamed and struggled, knowing that he was being carried off to death, and knowing that nothing he said or did would do any good. He must have asked them for something they had not approved of, Kyle realized, as the vampire's screams echoed throughout the chamber. Finally, a door opened, he was led outside, and the door slammed behind him. The room fell silent again.

Kyle could feel the tension in the air, as the other vampires looked at each other, dreading the moment of audience.

Kyle saw Lore approach an attendant, close to the Council, and whisper in his ear. The attendant, in turn, walked up to a judge, knelt down, and whispered in his ear.

The judge turned his head ever so slightly, and the man pointed, right to Kyle. Even from this great distance, Kyle could feel the judge's eyes bore into him, hidden in his hood. Despite himself, Kyle felt a shiver. Finally, he was in the presence of true evil.

The attendant nodded, and that was Kyle's cue.

Kyle pushed his way through the crowd, and walked right out to the center of the empty floor. He stood in the small circle in the center of the room—the spot. He knew that if he looked up, directly above his head would be the hole in the ceiling, the oculus, open to the sky. In the daytime, it allowed in a shaft of sunlight; now, at sunset, the light was filtered, and very weak. The room was lit mostly by torches.

Kyle knelt and bowed, waiting for them to address him, as was proper vampire etiquette.

"Kyle of the Blacktide Coven," a judge announced slowly. "You are bold to approach us unannounced. If your request does not meet our approval, you know that you risk the death penalty."

It was not a question; it was a statement. Kyle knew the consequences. But he didn't fear the outcome.

"I am aware, my master," Kyle said simply, and waited.

Finally, after a slight rustling, there came another pronouncement: "Then speak. What do you request of us?"

"I've come from another time. Two hundred years in the future."

A loud murmur rose throughout the room. An attendant banged on the floor with his staff three times, and screamed, "Silence!"

Finally, the room quieted down.

Kyle continued. "I do not time travel lightly, as none of us do. There was an urgency. In the future, in the time that I live, there will be a war—a glorious vampire war. It will begin in New York and spread from there. It is the vampire Apocalypse we have dreamed of. Our kind will finally be victorious. We will wipe out the entire human race and enslave them. We will also wipe out the benevolent vampire covens, anyone who stands in our way.

"I know, because I am the leader of this war."

There arose another loud murmur, followed by the banging of the staff.

"But my war is not complete," Kyle yelled over the din. "There remains but one thorn in my side, one person who can ruin everything we've achieved, who can ruin this glorious future for our race. She comes from a special lineage, and she has come back in time, likely to escape me. I've come back to find her, and to kill her once and for all. Until I do, the future remains uncertain for us all.

"I come before you today to ask permission to kill her, here in your place, and time. I also would like your assistance in finding her."

Kyle lowered his head again and waited. His heart beat faster, as he awaited their judgment. Of course, it would be in their best interest to help him, and he could see no reason why they wouldn't. But then again, these creatures, alive for millions of years, older even than he, were completely unpredictable. He never knew what agenda the twelve of them had, and their rulings always seemed as arbitrary as the wind.

He waited amidst the thick silence.

Finally, there was the clearing of a throat.

"We know of whom you speak, of course," came the gravelly voice of a judge. "You speak of Caitlin. Of what will be the Pollepel Coven. But who is, really, of a different, and far more powerful coven. Yes, she arrived in our time yesterday. Of course we know this. And if we wanted to kill her ourselves, don't you think that we would have?"

Kyle knew better than to respond. They needed their little point of pride. He would just let them finish their speech.

"But we do admire your determination, and your future war," the judge continued. "Yes, we admire it very much."

There was another moment of thick silence.

"We will let you track her down," continued the judge, "but if you find her, you will not kill her. You will capture her alive, and bring her back to us. We would rather enjoy killing her ourselves, and watching her die slowly. She will be a perfect candidate for the Games."

Kyle felt himself seething with rage. *The Games. Of course.* That was all that these sick, old vampires ever cared about. He remembered now. They converted the Coliseum into an arena for their sport, pitted vampire against vampire, vampire against human, vampire against beasts, and loved to watch them all tear themselves to pieces. It was cruel, and in his own way, Kyle admired it.

But it was not what he wanted for Caitlin. He wanted her dead. Period. Not that he minded her being tortured. But he didn't want to waste any time, to leave any room for chance. Of course, no one had ever escaped or survived the Games. But at the same time, one never knew what could happen.

"But, my masters," Kyle protested, "Caitlin, as you said, hails from a powerful lineage, and she is much more dangerous and elusive than you imagine. I request your permission to kill her instantly. There is too much at stake."

"You are still young," said another judge, "and so we will forgive your guessing our judgment. Anyone else, we would kill on the spot."

Kyle lowered his head. He realized he had gone too far. No one *ever* argued against the judges.

"She is in Assisi. That is where you will go next. Go quickly, and do not delay. Now that you've mentioned it, we quite look forward to watching her die before our eyes."

Kyle turned to go.

"And Kyle," one of them called.

He spun around.

The lead judge pulled back his hood, revealing the most grotesque face Kyle had ever seen, covered in bumps and lines and warts. He opened his mouth and smiled a hideous smile, showing yellow, sharp teeth, and shining black eyes. He grinned even wider: "Next time you show up unannounced, it will be *you* who dies slowly."

CHAPTER SIX

Caitlin flew over the idyllic Umbrian countryside, passing over hills and valleys, surveying the lush, green landscape in the early morning light. Spread out below her were small farming communities, small, stone cottages surrounded by hundreds of acres of land, smoke rising from their chimneys.

As she headed north, the landscape changed, shifting to the hills and valleys of Tuscany. As far as she looked, she saw vineyards, planted in the rolling hills, and workers with large straw hats already at work, tending the vines in the early morning. This country was incredibly beautiful, and a part of her wished that she could just descend right here, settle down and make herself at home in one of these small farm cottages.

But she had work to do. She continued on, flying further north, holding Rose tightly, curled up inside her shirt. Caitlin could feel that Venice was approaching, and she felt like a magnet drawn to it. The closer she came, the more she could feel her heart beat in anticipation; she could already sense people there that she once knew. She was still obscured as to who. She still couldn't sense whether Caleb was there, or whether he was even alive.

Caitlin had always dreamed of going to Venice. She had seen pictures of its canals, of gondolas, and had always imagined herself going there one day, maybe with someone she loved. She had even imagined herself being proposed to on one of those gondolas. But she had never expected to be going like this.

As she flew and flew, getting ever closer, it struck her that the Venice she'd be visiting now, in 1790, might be very different from the Venice she'd seen pictures of in the 21st century. It would probably, she imagined, be smaller, less developed, more rural. She also imagined that it would not be as crowded.

But she soon realized that she couldn't be more wrong.

As Caitlin finally reached the outskirts of Venice, she was shocked to see, even from this height, that the city beneath her looked startlingly similar to its pictures in modern times. She recognized the historic, famous architecture, recognized all the small bridges, recognized the same twists and turns to the canals. Indeed, she was shocked to realize that the Venice of 1790 was not, at least in outward appearances, all that different from the Venice of the 21st century.

The more she thought about it, the more it made sense. Venice's architecture was not just 100 or 200 years old: it was hundreds and hundreds of years old. She remembered a history class, in one of her many high schools, teaching about Venice, about some of its churches, built in the 12th century. Now she wished she had listened more carefully. The Venice below her, a sprawling, built-up mass of buildings, was not a brand-new city. It was, even in 1790, already several hundred years old.

Caitlin felt comforted by the fact. She had imagined that the year 1790 would be like a different planet, and she was relieved to know that some things actually hadn't changed that much. This looked to be essentially the same city she would have visited in the 21st century. The only immediate difference she could see was that its waterways did not contain a single motorized boat, of course. There were no speedboats, no large ferries, no cruise ships. Instead, the waterways were packed with huge sailing vessels, their masts climbing dozens of feet high.

Caitlin was also surprised by the crowds. She dove lower, now only a hundred feet over the city, and could see that even now, in the early morning, the streets were absolutely packed with people. And that the waterways were absolutely packed with boat traffic. She was shocked. This city was more congested than Times Square. She had always imagined that going back in history would mean fewer people, smaller crowds. She guessed she was wrong about that, too.

As she flew over it, as she circled it again and again, the thing that surprised her most, though, was that Venice was not just one city, just one island—it was spread out over many islands, dozens of islands stretching in every direction, each holding its own buildings, its own small city. The island on which Venice sat clearly held the most buildings, and was the most built-up. But the dozens of other islands all seemed interconnected, a vital part of the city.

The other thing that surprised her was the color of the water: a glowing, blue aqua. It was so light, so surreal, the kind of water she might have expected to find somewhere in the Caribbean.

As she circled over the islands, again and again, trying to orient herself, to figure out where to land, she regretted never having visited it in the 21st century. Well, at least she'd have a chance now.

Caitlin was also a bit overwhelmed. It seemed such a large, sprawling place. She had no idea where to set down, where to even begin to look for the people she might have once known—if they were even here. She had foolishly imagined Venice to be smaller, more quaint. Even from up here, she could already tell that she could walk this city for days and not go from one end to the other.

She realized that there would be no place to set down inconspicuously on the actual island of Venice. It was too crowded, and there was no way to approach it without being conspicuous. She didn't want to call that kind of attention to herself. She had no idea what other covens were down there, and how territorial they were; she had no idea if they were kind or malevolent; and she had no idea if the humans here, like those in Assisi, were on the lookout for vampires, and would hunt her down. The last thing she needed was another mob.

Caitlin decided to land on the mainland, far from the island. She noticed huge boats, filled with people, that seemed to be setting out from the mainland, and she figured that would be the best staging off point. At least the boats would take her right into the heart of the city.

Caitlin landed inconspicuously behind a grove of trees, on the mainland, not too far from the boats. She sat Rose down, who immediately ran to the closest bush and relieved herself. When she was done, Rose looked up at Caitlin and whined. Caitlin could see in her eyes that she was hungry. She empathized: she was, too.

The flying had tired her out, and Caitlin realized that she wasn't fully recovered yet. She also realized that she had worked up an appetite. She wanted to feed. And not on human food.

She looked around and saw no deer in sight. There wasn't time to go searching. A loud whistle came from the boat, and she felt it was about to depart. She and Rose would have to wait, and figure it out later.

With a pang, Caitlin felt homesick, missed the safety and comfort of Pollepel, missed being by Caleb's side, his teaching her how to hunt, his guiding her. By his side, she always felt that everything would be all right. Now, on her own, she wasn't so sure.

*

Caitlin walked, Rose by her side, to the closest boat. It was a large, sailing boat with a long rope ramp leading down to the shore, and as she looked up, she saw that it was completely packed with people. The final passengers were heading up the ramp, and Caitlin hurried up, with Rose, hurrying to get on before it was removed.

But she was surprised by a large, beefy hand, which slapped her hard on the chest, reaching out and stopping her.

"Ticket," came the voice.

Caitlin looked over and saw a big, muscular man scowling down at her. He was uncouth and unshaven, and he smelled even from here.

Caitlin's anger rose. She was already on edge from not eating, and she resented his hand stopping her.

"I don't have one," Caitlin snapped. "Can't you just let us on?"

The man shook his head firmly and turned away, ignoring her. "No ticket, no ride," he said.

Her anger rose another notch, and she forced herself to think of Aiden. What would he have told her? *Breathe deep. Relax. Use her mind, not your body.* He would have reminded her that she was stronger than this human. He would've told her to center herself. To focus. To use her *inner* talents.

She closed her eyes and tried to focus on her breathing. She tried to gather her thoughts, to direct them at this man.

You will let us on the boat, she willed. *You will do it without our paying you.*

Caitlin opened her eyes and expected him to be standing there, offering her passage. But, to her chagrin, he wasn't. He was still ignoring her, untying the last of the ropes.

It wasn't working. Either she had lost her mind control powers, or they hadn't fully come back yet. Or maybe she was just too frazzled, wasn't centered enough.

She suddenly remembered something. Her pockets. She quickly searched them, wondering what, if anything, she had brought back from the 21st century. She found something, and was relieved to see it was a $20 bill.

"Here," she said, handing it to him.

He took it, crumpled it, and held it up, examining it.

"What is this?" he asked. "I don't know this."

"It's a $20 bill," Caitlin explain, realizing, even as she explained it, how stupid she sounded. Of course. Why *would* he recognize it? It was American. And it wouldn't exist for another two hundred years.

With a pang of fear, Caitlin suddenly realize that all of the money she had on her would be useless.

"Garbage," he said, shoving it back into her hand.

Caitlin looked over and saw with a pang of fear that they were undoing the ropes, that the boat was preparing to depart. She thought quick, reached again into her pockets, and pulled out some change. She looked down, found a quarter, and reached out and handed it to him.

He took it, more interested, and held it up to the light. Still, though, he wasn't convinced.

He pushed it back into her palm.

"Come back with real money," he said; he also looked at Rose, and added, "and no dogs."

Caitlin's mind turned to Caleb. Maybe he was there, just out of her reach, on the island of Venice, just a boat ride away. She felt furious that this man was keeping her from him. She *had* the money—just not *his* money. Plus, the boat barely looked seaworthy, and it held hundreds of people. Did one more ticket really make such a big difference? It just wasn't fair.

As he stuck the money into Caitlin's palm, he suddenly clasped his big, sweaty hand over hers, and grabbed her wrist. He leered down and broke into a big, crooked smile, revealing several missing teeth. She could smell his bad breath.

"If you have no money, you pay me in other ways," he said, broadening his creepy smile, and as he did, he reached up with his other hand and touched her cheek.

Caitlin's reflexes kicked in, and she automatically reached up and swatted his hand away, hard, and extracted her wrist from his grasp. She was surprised by her own strength.

He looked back at her, apparently shocked that such a small girl would have such force, and his smile turned to an indignant scowl. He hocked up something from his throat, and then spit right at her feet. Caitlin looked down and saw it land on her shoes, and was revolted.

"You lucky I no cut you up," he grunted at her, then abruptly turned his back and went back to untying the ropes.

Caitlin felt her cheeks redden, as the rage overcame her. Were men the same everywhere? In every time and age? Was this a preview of what she could expect for the treatment of women in this time and place? She thought of all the other women out there, of everything that they must have had to put up with in this time, and she felt her anger grow. She felt like she needed to stand up for all of them.

He was still bent over, untying the ropes, and she quickly leaned back and kicked the brute hard, right on his butt. The kick sent him flying over the peer, head first, right into the water, fifteen feet below. He landed with a loud splash.

Caitlin quickly ran up the rope ramp, Rose by her side, and pushed her way onto the huge sailing ship, packed with people.

It had happened so fast, no one, she hoped, had seen it. That seemed to be the case, as the crew pulled in the roped walkway, and the ship began to set sail.

Caitlin hurried to the edge and looked down: she could see him splashing in the water, bobbing his head up, as he raised a fist up at the boat.

"Stop boat! Stop boat!" the man screamed.

His cries were drowned out, though, as hundreds of excited passengers cheered at the boat's finally setting sail.

One of the crew noticed him, though, and ran over to the side of the boat, following the man's finger, as he pointed towards Caitlin.

Caitlin didn't wait to see what happened. She quickly ducked into the thick of the crowd, Rose at her side, ducking and weaving this way and that, until she was deep in the center of the boat, in the thick of the masses. She pushed deeper, and kept moving. There were hundreds of people crammed together, and she hoped they wouldn't spot her, or Rose.

Within minutes, the boat was gaining speed. After a while, Caitlin finally breathed deep. She realized that no one was coming after her, or, as far as she could tell, even searching for her.

She began to cut her way through the crowd more calmly, Rose beside her, heading towards the far side of the boat. She finally made it, squeezed her way beside the crowded railing, and leaned over and looked.

In the distance, the brute was still bobbing in the water, pulling himself up onto the dock—but by now he was just a dot on the horizon. Caitlin smiled. Served him right.

She turned the other way and saw that Venice loomed straight ahead.

She smiled wider, leaning over and feeling the cool seawater pushing back her hair. It was a warm day in May, and the temperature was perfect, and the salt air refreshing. Rose jumped up beside her, pressing her paws on the edge of the railing, and looked out and smelled the air, too.

Caitlin had always loved boats. She had never visited an authentic, historic sailing ship—much less, sailed on one. She smiled and corrected herself: this was no longer a *historic* ship. It was a modern one. It was 1790 after all. She almost laughed aloud at the thought.

She looked up at the tall wooden masts, rising into the sky. She watched as the sailors all lined up and heaved on the thick ropes; as they did, yard and yards of heavy canvas were raised, and she could heard the flapping of the material. It looked heavy, and the sailors sweated in the sun, yanking the ropes with all they had just to raise the canvas a few inches.

So this was how it was done. Caitlin was impressed by the efficiency of it all, by how seamlessly it worked. She couldn't believe how fast this huge, crowded boat was moving, especially without the benefit of modern engines. She wondered what the captain of the ship would do if she told him about 21st century engines, about how much faster he could go. He'd probably think she was crazy.

She looked down and saw, about twenty feet below, the water rushing by her, small waves lapping against the side of the boat. The water was so light, so blue, it was magical.

All around her, people squeezed in, all trying to make their way to the railing and look out. She looked around and realized how simply most of them were dressed, many in tunics and sandals, and some barefoot. Others, though, were dressed elegantly, and seemed to try to keep away from the masses. A few people wore elaborate masks, with a long, beaked nose. They laughed and jostled each other, and seemed drunk.

In fact, as she looked, she noticed that a good portion of the passengers were swigging from bottles of wine and seemed drunk, even in the early morning. The entire boat, now that she noticed it, had a festive, rowdy atmosphere, as if they were all on their way to a giant party.

Caitlin pushed her way along the railing, through the crowd, past parents holding up children, and slowly but surely made her way to the front. Finally, she had the view she wanted. She leaned over the edge, and watched as the boat bore down directly on Venice.

The unimpeded site of the city took her breath away. She could see its outline, the beautiful, historic buildings, all lined up neatly next to each other, all built to face the water. Some of the facades were really grand, ornate, their white façades covered in all sorts of moldings and details. Many had arched walls and arched windows open to the water, and, amazingly, had their main entry doors right at water level. It was incredible. One could literally pull right up to one's front door by boat and step inside.

Amidst all the buildings, there were spires rising from churches, and occasional domes punctuating the horizon. This was a city of magnificent architecture, of a grand, ornate style, and it all seemed designed to face the water. It did not merely co-exist with the water—it embraced it.

And all along it, connecting one side of the city to the other, were small, arched footbridges, steps rising up each side and a wide plateau in the middle. These were crowded with people walking up and down or just sitting on the edge, watching all the ships as they passed by.

And everywhere—*everywhere*—there were ships. The canals were absolutely crammed with traffic, with ships of every shape and size—so much so, that she could hardly see the water. The famous gondolas were everywhere, too, their oarsmen standing on the edge, steering them in the water. She was surprised by how long they were, some seeming to stretch nearly 30 feet. In between these were smaller ships and boats of all sorts, some for delivering food, some for taking out waste. This place was alive, bustling. She had never seen anything like it in her life.

As she surveyed the crowds, the masses of humanity, she felt a chill in her spine, as she wondered if Caleb could be among them. Could she be looking at him right now? She knew was being foolish, especially from so far away, but still, she tried to look, to scan their faces, to see if maybe, just maybe, she could spot him.

As Caitlin took in the magnitude, the immensity of the city, the thousands of people swarming in every direction, a part of her, the intellectual part, felt hopeless. She realized that this was a futile mission, that there was no possible way she could ever find Caleb among all these people. But another part of her, the part of her that believed in destiny, felt excited, felt optimistic, just *knew* that somehow, deep down, if Caleb were here, they would find each other.

And either way, she could not help but feel the thrill of adventure and excitement. She was traveling. Journeying around the world. About to experience a new city.

And maybe, just maybe, Caleb would be on its shores.

*

Caitlin filed off the boat with the hundreds of other passengers, squeezed between them as she worked her way, Rose beside her, down the steep rope ramp. It was utter chaos. By now, most, if not all, of the passengers were rowdy and drunk, and it was a free-for-all getting to the dock.

Caitlin was relieved when her feet touched the ground, and she quickly guided Rose with her away from the thick crowd, off the dock, and onto the streets of Venice.

It was overwhelming. Caitlin had hoped that once she got away from the boat, that the crowds would ease up—but that was hardly the case. There were crowds everywhere. She was getting jostled left and right.

She found herself in an enormous open square, around which were built immense buildings, all facing it. She read the sign: Piazza San Marco. St. Mark's Square. Dominating the square was an enormous church, the Basilica di San Marco, and across from it was an immense, skinny tower, reaching hundreds of feet into the sky, The Campanile. As if on cue, the huge church bell tolled, and the sound filled the square like a bomb.

Thousands of people milled about, engaging in a dizzying array of activity. As she ventured tentatively out into the square, strangers approached her from every direction, all trying to sell their wares. They held out small, wooden dolls, brightly colored glass, flasks of wine, and most of all, masks. Everywhere she looked, there were masks. Even stranger, everywhere she looked, she was shocked to see people wearing them. The predominant mask was white, with a long, beaked nose, but there were masks of all shapes and sizes. Even stranger, many people walked about in full costume, some fully cloaked. It was as if she'd arrived in one huge Halloween party. She had no idea what the occasion was. Did people here always dress like this?

As if that were not enough, everyone seemed to be drunk, or quickly getting drunk. People laughed too loud, sang songs to themselves, jostled each other, and openly drank from jugs of wine. There was music everywhere, every few feet another guitarist, or violinist, sitting on a crate or stool, playing away with an open hat and asking for tips.

Completing the scene were jugglers, comics, clowns, and performers of all sorts. Before her, one man juggled brightly colored balls, while another man juggled torches of fire. Caitlin stopped, in awe, watching.

She was soon jostled roughly, and turned to see a large man, dressed in a cloak and mask, drunk, stumbling, his arm around an elaborately dressed courtesan. As Caitlin watched, he reached down and grabbed her rear roughly, and she screamed with laughter.

This city was like a circus. It was the rowdiest, most chaotic place she had ever seen. She marveled that all this licentiousness could be taking place right here, in front of these churches. It was the strangest dichotomy she had ever seen. Was the city just one, endless party? Or had she arrived at some special time?

Caitlin spotted a small group of finely dressed woman cutting their way through the crowd. They were each dressed in elaborate gowns, ruffling their way, and held a small pouch to their noses as they went.

Caitlin wondered what they were holding, and at just that moment, it hit her. The stench. She had been too stunned to notice it at first, but now, as she walked, she was overwhelmed by the horrible smell of everyone and everything around her. It smelled like no one here had bathed. Ever.

And then she remembered: of course, no one had. It was 1790, after all. Plumbing hadn't been invented yet. As the sun grew higher, and the temperature grew warmer, the stench grew even worse. Caitlin held her nose, but no matter which way she turned, she couldn't get away from it. That's why those women were holding those pouches to their noses: to block out the smell.

Caitlin suddenly felt claustrophobic, and spotted what looked like a side street; she cut her way through a group of jugglers and guitar players, and as she crossed the square, she saw that there were many side streets leading in and out of the square. They were more like narrow alleyways, underneath arched buildings, and she ducked into the nearest one.

Finally, she could breathe; Rose looked relieved, too. They headed down the narrow side street, and it weaved its way left and right. The streets were so narrow, and the buildings blocked out most of the light, and she began to feel confined in this city. She stood there, debating which way to go. She had barely ventured a few blocks, and already she felt disoriented, turned around. She had no idea where she was going, or where to look for Caleb—if he was even here. She wished she had a map—but then again, she had no money—or, at least, no *real* money—to pay for one.

Worse, she felt the hunger gnawing away at her again, and felt herself growing more irritable. Rose, as if reading her mind, whined. The poor thing was hungry, too. Caitlin was determined to find a way to get them both food.

She suddenly heard a wooden shutter opening up above, followed by a loud splashing. She jumped back, as a bucket of water hit the ground, close to her, startling her. She looked up and saw an old woman, missing teeth, looking down as she finished emptying a bucket, and then slammed closed the shutters.

Caitlin smelled a horrible stench, and didn't need anyone to explain to her what the woman had just done: thrown a bucket of urine out the window. She was revolted. She heard another shutter opening, in the distance, and looked over and watched someone else do the same. She looked down and realized that the streets were lined with urine and feces. She also noticed several rats scurrying to and fro. She nearly wretched. It made her, for the first time, really appreciate the inventions and comforts of her time that she had always taken for granted. Plumbing. Sewage systems. She longed for cleanliness, and felt more homesick than ever. If this was a sneak preview of urban life in 1790, she wasn't sure she could handle it.

Caitlin hurried along, before any more shutters opened, and finally saw what looked like an opening up ahead. She reached the end of the alleyway, and it indeed opened up onto another square, this one less crowded. She was relieved to be out of the side streets and back out into the open light and air again.

She crossed the square, and sat on the edge of the large, circular fountain, in one of the few empty seats amidst the crowd. Rose jumped up beside her, and sat looking up at her, whining.

As Caitlin sat there, trying to collect her thoughts, a person approached, holding out a canvas and pointing at it with a paintbrush. She looked up at him, puzzled, and he kept pointing. "I draw your picture," he said. "Very pretty. Very nice. You pay me."

Caitlin shook her head. "I'm sorry," she said. "I don't have any money."

The man quickly hurried off. Caitlin looked around the square, and noticed street artists everywhere, all trying to get people to pay them. And then she noticed something which alarmed her: packs of wild dogs. They combed along the sides of the square, rifling through trash, and she saw one dog stop and look her way. It seemed to focus on Rose—and soon, it was trotting in their direction.

Rose must have sensed it, too, because she turned slowly and faced the oncoming animal. Caitlin could feel Rose tense up, and she tensed, too. The large, mangy dog looked somewhat like a German Shepherd, and it came up to Rose, and sniffed her. Rose sniffed back, her hair standing up on her back; as the dog tried to walk behind Rose, Rose suddenly snapped, snarling with an unearthly noise, baring her teeth, and biting the dog's neck—hard.

The dog yelped. Although it was bigger, Rose was clearly more powerful and she did not let go. Finally, the dog took off.

Rose, worked up, sat there, snarling, a vicious, unearthly sound, and several people backed away, giving them space.

Caitlin was shocked. She had never seen Rose like that before. It made her realize Rose was not the small, innocent pup she remembered; she was growing up, and would soon be a full-bred wolf, and a force to be reckoned with.

Caitlin felt the unwelcome stares in their direction, and decided to move on, before someone realized that Rose was not just another dog. The last thing she wanted was to call more attention to them.

Caitlin got up and led Rose to the opposite side of the square. She looked at all the side streets and alleyways leading into and out of the square, and felt overwhelmed. Had she been foolish to come here? How could she ever possibly find Caleb amidst these masses, in this maze of a city? Maybe she should have followed the Priest's advice, and gone to Florence instead. Had she been foolish to follow her heart?

Before she could finish the thought, something caught her attention. On the far side of the square, she noticed a girl get dragged down an alleyway, and heard her muffled cry, before a hand was clasped over her mouth. Clearly, she was in trouble.

Without thinking, Caitlin sprang into action, chasing towards her.

She ran into the alleyway, Rose by her side, and soon found herself running down a set of twisting and turning alleys. She heard the muffled cries in the distance, and turned down another alleyway, then another, getting lost in the maze of narrow side streets.

Finally, she spotted the girl up ahead. She was being dragged by three men towards the end of an alley, one of them with a hand over her mouth, and the others each grabbing an arm. They were huge men, all bald, covered in scars, and evil-looking.

The girl fought back valiantly, biting one of their hands, eyes open wide in fear as she jerked her arms and elbows and legs—but it was of little use. These men were clearly stronger than her.

"Let her go!" Caitlin screamed, as she ran towards them and stopped.

The three men stopped, turned, and looked at Caitlin. They must have been shocked to see a single girl confronting them. At first, they didn't know what to make of it.

"I said, let her go," Caitlin said, in a low, steely voice. "I'm not going to tell you again."

Caitlin thought back to the all the times in her life when she'd been bullied, overpowered, especially when she'd been human. She hated bullies, more than anything. And if there was anything she hated worse than that, it was seeing a guy trying to hurt a girl. She felt the rage overwhelm her, felt the heat rise up from her toes, up through her legs and shoulders and hands; she felt it transform her, give her power she never knew she had. It was blinding, all-encompassing. She had no choice. It drove her.

The three cretins dropped the girl, roughly, on the stone, smiled at each other, and turned and walked towards Caitlin. The girl could have ran, but instead she stayed where she was, watching. Caitlin heard Rose growl beside her.

Caitlin didn't wait. She took three steps forward, leapt into the air, and planted two feet hard on the lead man's chest, kicking him so hard that he flew back several feet.

Before the others could react, she wheeled and elbowed one hard across the face, cracking his cheek with a loud noise, and sending him to the ground.

The third man grabbed her from behind with all he had. Caitlin struggled, surprised for a moment. This one was much stronger than she'd expected.

Just as she prepared to flip him over her shoulder, she heard the sound of breaking glass, and felt him drop his grip.

She turned and saw the girl standing behind her, a broken bottle in her hand, and the man lying limp on the ground: she had clearly smashed a bottle over his head.

Before Caitlin could thank her, the first man, back on his feet, charged at her again. But Rose was mad now, and she took the lead, charging him, leaping into the air, and clamping down hard on his throat. The man dropped to the ground, squirming and screaming, but he could not get Rose off.

Finally, he passed out, and Rose returned to Caitlin's side.

Caitlin surveyed the damage: the three men lay there, unconscious.

She turned and looked at the girl.

The girl stared back, bewildered and grateful at the same time.

Caitlin stared back at her, and Caitlin was shocked, too. But not because of what had happened.

Rather, because she *knew* this girl.

In fact, she had once been her best friend.

It was Polly.

CHAPTER SEVEN

Sam woke to the sound of clanging church bells. He never knew bells could ring that loudly, and he felt as if he were inside the bell itself. His entire body shook with the sound, as he opened his eyes to utter blackness. He reached out, and felt stone in front of him.

He frantically reached out in every direction, and felt himself encased in stone. He was flat on his back. He tried to move side to side, but couldn't, and that's when he realized: he was in a coffin.

Panicking, Sam reached up with all his might, and after several seconds, was finally able to move the stone lid; with a scraping noise, it slid just a few inches, as light and fresh air poured in through the crack. He breathed deeply, realizing how badly he needed it.

He slid a few fingers into the crack, and with all his might, pushed the lid to the side. Again it scraped, protesting, but soon he was able to get all his fingers in, then his hands. Within moments, he pushed the stone lid completely off, and with one final heave, it crashed to the floor, cracking into a million pieces.

He sat upright, gasping for air, and shielded his eyes from the light.

Sam jumped up from the coffin, and, stumbling on weak legs, scurried over to the corner, hiding from the direct sunlight. He searched his pockets, and quickly unraveled his skin wraps, and wrapped his arms and shoulders. He found the eye drops in his pocket, too, and put two in each eye.

After a moment, his breathing relaxed. He started to calm, to feel himself again. He looked around.

He was in a tomb of some sort, an ancient, dusty tomb. He saw an open door, leading outside.

Sam steeled himself and walked out, into the sunlight, and realized with a shock where he was. At the top of a hill, exiting a church's mausoleum, spread out before him were hundreds of steps, leading down to a city. Rome. The entire city spread out before him, and he was afforded a magnificent view. He turned and examined the church he exited from, then turned back, and looked again at the steps. It all suddenly struck him. He knew where he was. He had seen this picture many times on postcards: the Spanish steps of Rome.

His time travel had worked. He didn't know exactly why it had taken him to this place, or what year it was, but he hoped it would be the same year that Kyle had gone to. Sam couldn't remember much—his entire time in New York now felt hazy, like a dream—but he did remember one thing: his single-minded pursuit of Kyle. He remembered finding out that Kyle had gone back in time to kill his sister, and that once he learned this, he couldn't rest. He was determined to find Kyle, no matter what it took, and kill him before he could harm his sister.

Before he'd discovered this news, Sam has been depressed, at odds, in a deep despair for what he'd done to his sister, and to Caleb. He had never meant any of it. Once he'd found out what Kyle was up to, he'd seen this as his chance to make amends for all that he had done—and to avenge himself on Kyle. Sam knew that he could never expect the forgiveness of Caitlin. But at the very least, perhaps, he could help her in his own, small way.

As Sam descended the steps, through the mobs of people, he noticed several of them parting ways for him, looking at him funny. Some of them were pointing at him, then looking up the hill. He suddenly realized that he must have made an odd site, probably covered in dust from the tomb. And some of them may have seen him exiting right from the mausoleum, and had probably heard the shattering of stone.

He quickened his pace, figuring it best not to let them wonder too much, and headed off down the stairs at a quick jog, taking them three at a time.

Sam weaved his way through the crowd, wondering which way to go. He could feel Kyle's presence strongly in the city. It was hard *not* to feel it—the man emanated evil, oozed it in a tangible trail. Sam followed the trail, following his senses, as he navigated down the side streets of Rome. He barely took in any of the scene before him, as he was so single-mindedly focused on completing his mission.

Sam felt himself gravitating down a particular street, then down a particular alleyway.

He stopped just in time, nearly tripping: there, beneath him, were two rotting corpses, one of what looked like a prostitute, and the other of a man that looked like her pimp. He sensed strongly that Kyle had been here, and had done this.

Sam followed his senses down several more side streets, and before he knew it, he found himself entering in a large, ancient square: The

Piazza Della Rotonda. And there, before him, was the place he sought: the Pantheon.

Sam stared in awe. It was magnificent. With its his huge columns spread out before its entranceway, its circular dome, it was both beautiful and imposing. He had seen it before online, but it had been nothing compared to seeing it in person.

Online, he thought, and nearly laughed aloud. He looked around carefully for the first time, saw the people dressed in ancient garb, saw the lack of cars and any modern conveniences, and marveled at how many years these people were from knowing what online meant.

Sam focused. He sensed Kyle behind those walls. He tightened his fist, preparing for battle.

Sam took off at a sprint for the structure. He felt deep down that he was at least as strong as Kyle, and if he was going to die fighting him, better to get it over with.

Sam ran up the steps and put his shoulder into the huge, open doors; oddly, they were already ajar, as if waiting.

He found himself running down the corridor and right into the center of the main, circular room of the Pantheon. He braced himself, ready for a fight, ready to confront Kyle, ready to go down swinging.

But as he finished charging into the room, as he stopped and looked around, to his surprise, he saw that the room was completely empty. His footsteps echoed off the walls, off the huge dome ceiling, off the marble floor, as he turned in every direction, looking for Kyle, looking for any adversary.

He was stunned. He'd felt certain that Kyle was here, and had never before been so misled by his senses. Was this some sort of trick?

Before he could finish the thought, Sam suddenly felt something moving towards him, impossibly fast, and at the last second, he looked up to see what it was. Hundreds of vampires, their wings out spread like bats, had been clinging to the ceiling, waiting for him.

They now all dropped like spiders, diving right for him, hundreds of them, only feet away.

It was too late for him to react. All Sam could see was the terrible blackness of hundreds of vampires descending, eager to devour its prey. Their squeals and snarls were horrible, and as their huge wings wrapped around him from every direction, he could not help but wonder if this would be the last thing he saw on earth.

CHAPTER EIGHT

Caitlin stood there, stunned. She could not believe that it was really Polly. She looked exactly the same as she had, with her distinctive translucent white skin, her light brown hair, and her blue eyes, large and shining. She also looked the same age, somewhere around 18. Rationally, Caitlin knew that she should have expected this; but seeing it face to face threw her completely off guard.

Polly broke into a wide smile, grinning from ear to ear, displaying her beautiful, white teeth—the exact smile that Caitlin remembered. It was uncanny. And it felt so good to recognize someone. For the first time, Caitlin didn't feel so alone.

"Well, you sure know how to fight, don't you?" Polly asked. It was the same accent, the same voice, the same mannerisms. Polly examined Caitlin for a moment, and something like recognition seemed to cross her face, and then quickly went away.

"I'm Polly," she said, extending her hand. "And to whom do I owe the pleasure?"

Caitlin didn't know what to say. She was really shocked. If there was anything more uncanny than seeing Polly again, it was having Polly not recognize her, as if she were a complete stranger, as if they had never met, never shared any of their experiences on Pollepel.

Of course, Caitlin knew there was no reason why Polly *would* remember her; after all, Caitlin had come *back* in time, not forwards. Still, Caitlin had known her so well, so vividly. It was completely eerie. She almost wondered if Polly were kidding, just testing her?

Caitlin reached out and shook her hand.

"Polly," she said, "it's me. Caitlin."

Polly stared back, and her face wrinkled in confusion. Finally, Caitlin realized that it was true: Polly really had no idea who she was.

"I'm sorry," Polly answered, "have we met? I'm afraid I don't recall. Forgive me if we have. I am terrible with names and faces. Caitlin is your name? That's a pretty one. Anyway, now that we've *officially* met, I'm sure glad to meet you. You really saved me," Polly said, surveying the three unconscious brutes, still lying in the alley. "They were a rotten sort."

Rose came running over to Polly, whining and wagging her tail hysterically.

Polly's eyes opened wide in delight, as she bent over and petted her. "And what have we here?" she asked.

"Her name is Rose," Caitlin said. It was clear Rose remembered Polly, and it was equally clear that Polly didn't remember her.

Still, Polly showed Rose as much affection as she once had.

"Rose," Polly said, hugging her as Rose licked her cheek. "What a darling name." Polly laughed. "Now now, Rose!" Polly said. "My God, she's so excited! You'd think that she knew me!"

Caitlin smiled. "Yes, you would think," she said.

One of the unconscious men groaned, and Polly suddenly surveyed the alleyway. "Let's get out of here," she said, and took Caitlin's arm in hers, and guided her out the alleyway, Rose by their side.

They walked, arm in arm, like new best friends, down the side streets of Venice, Polly leading the way. Polly was so happy, she was practically skipping, and Caitlin was thrilled to see how happy Rose was. Even though Polly didn't remember, it still felt like they knew each other forever. Just like the first time they'd met in Pollepel.

"I don't know how to repay you," Polly said. "Those men didn't mean me the best, to put it lightly. It's my own fault, really. Aiden warned us to never venture out alone. Safety in numbers, that's what he says. I'm strong—don't think I'm not—but today I'm not at my full strength, and they caught me off guard. I'm much stronger at night. It would've ended badly, I'm sure of it. At the very least, it would have put me out of commission for tonight, and that simply wouldn't do."

Caitlin tried to keep up. Just as she remembered, Polly talked so fast, she could barely get a word in. It warmed her heart to be back with her, to be back by her best friend's side, even if Polly couldn't remember. She hoped that maybe, over time, Polly would remember. If not, she'd be more than happy to begin their friendship all over again.

More importantly, Caitlin was struck by her reference. Had she said *Aiden*? Could it be?

"Did you say Aiden?" Caitlin asked.

"Why yes," Polly said. "Do you know him? Of course, there's no way you could. You haven't been to our island, have you? No, no, of course not. I would have known, of course. But you'll see it now. I have to introduce you to everyone. Humans are not allowed, of course. Just our kind," Polly said, looking over at Caitlin. "Of course, I can sense you're one of us. I knew the second I saw you."

Caitlin tried to speak, but Polly cut her off.

"You don't have a coven here, do you? Of course you don't. I know every vampire in town." She grabbed her arm, pleading, "You *have* to join ours. You *have* to! I'll talk to Aiden. I'm sure he'll let you in, especially after he hears how you saved me. Oh, I can't thank you enough! Talk about timing. It's like it was destined."

Polly led them down an alleyway, into another small square, then down another side street, and underneath a small, stone arch. Caitlin found herself crossing over a foot bridge, over a narrow canal, and then back down the other side. Polly seemed to really know the back streets.

Caitlin thought. It was always hard to gather her thoughts around Polly.

"Polly," she said, trying to catch her breath, "you said you know every vampire in town?"

"Well, I wouldn't say *every*, but most of them, for sure. Venice is bigger than you think. Has loads and loads of islands, and some, I hear, hide out on small islands I've never heard of."

Caitlin's heart pounded with excitement. "Have you heard of Caleb?" she asked.

Polly furrowed her brow.

"Caleb…I'm sorry, that's not ringing a bell…No, can't say that I know him."

Caitlin's heart fell. Maybe he really hadn't survived the trip. Maybe her sensing friends in Venice only had to do with Polly. Maybe Caleb really was gone.

"So, will you?" Polly asked

Caitlin looked at her, puzzled. "Will I what?"

"Come with me? To our island? It would be so fun. *Please*. I can use the companionship. It gets so *boring* there. And I can hardly let you just go, especially after all that. Come on, you don't have any other place to go, do you? *Please*, make a girl happy."

Caitlin thought. She didn't see why not. After all, she had nowhere else to go. And she really wanted to spend more time with Polly, too—and meet Aiden again.

Caitlin smiled. "Sure. I'd love to."

Polly squealed in delight. "Perfect! We have an extra room, just for you. Great views of the water. Right next to mine. And Rose," Polly added, bending over and petting her, "of course, there's a room for you, too."

Rose wagged her tail, and then started whining hysterically.

"Oh, poor dear," Polly said, "she's ravished, isn't she? And you look ravished, too."

Polly yanked her down a side alleyway, and Caitlin was disoriented, barely able to keep up with all the twists and turns. She wondered how she would've found her in way Venice without her.

Polly stopped before a villager roasting a pig, slicing off pieces and selling it to customers.

Rose smacked her lips at the sight.

"Two, please," Polly said, reaching into her pocket and handing the woman a coin. "And one jug of your special," she winked.

The woman nodded back knowingly. She sliced two huge hunks of meat, and handed them to Caitlin. She then handed Caitlin a small, ceramic jug.

Caitlin reached down and fed the strips to Rose.

Rose, famished, could hardly wait. She leapt up and ate them in the air, and devoured them, smacking her lips. She immediately whined for more, staring hopefully at Caitlin.

Polly laughed. "OK, Rose, I get it," she said, and handed the woman another coin. An even larger slice of meat came off the pig, and Polly gave it to Rose with a laugh.

Caitlin examined the jug. It was filled with a dark, thick liquid.

"Drink it," Polly said. "You'll be happy you did. It's just for our kind."

"What is it?" Caitlin asked, unsure.

"Blood," Polly answered. "Not of humans, don't worry. Of deer. The woman keeps a stock just for us."

Caitlin didn't like the smell, but she was overwhelmed with hunger pangs, and she finally leaned back and drank.

As the blood coursed through her system, she felt renewed. She realized how ravished she'd been. She leaned back and chugged it, drinking and drinking, unable to stop herself. It dripped down her chin, as she downed the entire jug.

Polly laughed.

Caitlin wiped her mouth, self-conscious.

"Sorry," Caitlin said. "I guess I was hungry."

Caitlin felt her full strength returning, surging through every pore of her body. She felt reborn.

"It's the least I can do," Polly said. "After all, you saved a girl's life."

*

Polly led Caitlin through street after street in Venice, and finally, before them was open sky. Caitlin was in awe as she found herself at the waterfront, looking out at the Grand Canal of Venice, bustling with boat traffic in every direction. The salt breezes swept her face and hair, and it felt refreshing.

Polly didn't waste any time. She hurried to the waterside, and began untying a rope holding in place a long, black, gondola.

"Jump in!" Polly said.

Caitlin hesitated, unsure. It was such a long and narrow boat, so low to the water, and it rocked wildly in the rough waters, which were filled with enormous ships moving quickly in every direction. She could easily envision one of them running over a gondola.

"Oh it's fine," Polly said, reading her mind, "I'm in it all the time. Best mode of transportation, you know."

Polly held out a hand, and Caitlin took it as she balanced, stepping tentatively into the boat; it rocked wildly as she did.

Caitlin slid up, sitting hesitantly on the wooden plank, a bit wet from all the water spray.

Polly laughed. "You can tackle an alleyway full of men, but you're scared of a little boat?" Then she added, "Come on Rose! Your turn!"

Rose, still unsure, stood on the edge of the dock, staring at Caitlin for reassurance.

Caitlin nodded, and Rose ran and jumped into the boat, rocking it again.

She got her coat wet, and she shook it wildly, spraying both Caitlin and Polly.

They both laughed.

Polly finished untying the boat, got in herself, and stood in the back of it. She grabbed the long, wooden oar, and pushed off.

They were soon gliding through the water, and Caitlin was surprised at the boat's seaworthiness. They were so low in the water, it seemed as if the ocean might come in at any moment, and yet the boat must have been designed well, because they cut through it with a lot of speed, as Polly rowed. Caitlin settled in, and even with the rough waters rocking them, tried to relax.

A huge ship sailed past them, just a few feet away, and left a big wake. The gondola rocked even more wildly, and Caitlin sat up again.

Polly laughed. "You get used to it," she said.

Caitlin started to wonder exactly how far they were going.

"Where are we going, exactly?" Caitlin asked

"I live on Isola di San Michele," Polly said, "also known as Isle of the Dead. It's one of the outer islands of Venice, in the lagoon. Not too far. No one bothers us there, and we don't bother anyone. Plus, we have loads of livestock to feed on."

Isle of the Dead, Caitlin thought. It was interesting to see that Polly's coven still lived on an island, even these hundreds of years back. She wondered if it was anything like Pollepel. If it was, she'd be thrilled to be there.

"So why were you in Venice today?" Caitlin asked.

Polly sighed. "My fault. I should have brought backup. Aiden warned us not to travel alone. But I had to get something for tonight's party and no one was around. I just *had* to get the right dress. I have absolutely nothing to wear. I mean, I do, but nothing spectacular enough, at least not for tonight. I mean this ball only comes around once a year."

"Ball?" Caitlin asked.

"How can you not know!?" Polly asked, flabbergasted. "It's only the Grand Ball. I've been looking forward to it all year. I just wanted to sneak into town to see if I could find something better. I'm weaker in the day. I'm still training. If those guys got me at night, they would have paid. But like I said, they caught me off guard. Anyway, where did you learn to fight like that?"

"Oh," Caitlin said, smiling, "I learned a trick or two on an island once."

She was hoping that somehow Polly would catch the reference, would remember. But she didn't.

"An island? Do I know it? Near Venice?

Caitlin smiled.

"Not exactly," she said.

They rode the rest of the way in silence, Rose resting her head in Caitlin's lap.

Caitlin tried to collect her swirling thoughts as she anxiously looked out at the horizon, waiting for the first sign of land. She was excited to see where Polly lived, excited to see if there was anyone else there that she remembered. She hoped, prayed, that one of them had heard something, anything, about Caleb.

*

It was afternoon by the time they reached the small island, and it was lit up in a soft, orange glow. Caitlin could already tell it was beautiful. It was hardly bigger than Pollepel, stretching only a half a mile in each direction, but, unlike Pollepel, it was flat as a pancake. The trees here were different, too, with the tall, narrow Italian Cypress trees dotting the island, spread out everywhere amidst the lush, verdant grass. There was no grand castle, either, but instead, there was a huge, Renaissance church,

108

it's glowing white façade built right up against the water, facing the canal. It appeared to be hundreds of years old. Its entrance was flush against the water, and one could boat right up to the front doors, and step right in. She had seen this with other buildings in Venice, but it still amazed her, the idea that she could open a door and step right into the water.

Attached to the church was a huge cloister, stretching as far back as Caitlin could see, with a sloping, red-tiled roof, and dozens of arched walls and columns. Caitlin could already feel that Polly's coven lived here.

It was still hard for Caitlin to reconcile, the idea of vampires living inside a church, or cloister. She wondered why they had chosen this place, this island in the middle of nowhere. She assumed they could have chosen any place in Venice to live.

"Because it keeps us anonymous," Polly said, reading her mind. Caitlin reddened, always forgetting how adept vampires were at reading minds.

"Being here keeps us off the beaten path," Polly continued. "Venetians rarely trek out here, and when we visit them, we keep a low profile. It suits us both perfectly. We stay out of each other's hair."

They approached a low, gated entrance, on top of which stood several vampire guards, standing watch. Polly looked up and waved, but they stared down, straight-faced. Caitlin looked closely, but didn't recognize any of them.

"Open the gate," Polly said, annoyed.

"Who's she?" one of them asked, nodding at Caitlin.

"She's one of ours," Polly said.

"I don't recognize her," said the other.

"Just open the gate," Polly snapped. "I'm telling you it's fine. If you have a problem with it, take it up with Aiden."

They both paused, looking at each other, unsure. Finally, one of them pulled a lever, and the iron gate slowly rose up.

They boated right through, and onto the other side.

Caitlin looked around in amazement. This place was beautiful. In the fields, she could see dozens of vampires training in mock combat.

"Why this island?" Caitlin asked.

Polly looked at her.

"I mean, it seems like Venice has dozens of islands to choose from."

"This is a very special place," Polly said. "We have buried our dead here for thousands of years. It is the Isle of the Dead for more reasons than one."

Polly gave one last hard row, and their gondola pulled up right to the church door, its long wooden bow hitting the stone with a bang that shook the entire boat.

Rose ran down the length of it, and leapt onto the dock. Polly threw a rope onto a beam, pulled them in tight, and tied them up. Caitlin steadied herself, slowly standing in the vessel, which rocked as she did, and climbed onto shore.

Rose ran to the nearest bush and relieved herself, while Polly nimbly climbed out of the boat and finished tying the boat. She then opened wide the large church doors and stepped aside for them to enter.

Caitlin stepped inside, and was overwhelmed. Like the church in Assisi, this one had high, soaring ceilings, elaborately decorated with frescoes, and the open room was enormous. Light streamed in through the stained-glass windows, and as they walked down the marble aisle, their footsteps echoed all around them.

"The church of San Michele," Polly said, as they walked. "Its namesake, of course, is Saint Michael, the holder of the scales on Judgment Day. Legend has it that Saint Michael is the guardian of sleep for the faithful dead. One could hardly find a more appropriate place for us."

Polly led them to the back of the church, through a rear door, and it opened up onto a large, medieval courtyard. Columns stretched in every direction. It was solemn, and very peaceful, except for the two vampires sparring in the center, fighting with wooden swords, the click-clack of their swords echoing off the walls.

Caitlin stared at them, and couldn't believe it: Tyler and Taylor. The twins. They looked exactly as they had on Pollepel, identical brother and sister, startlingly attractive, they still looked to be maybe 16.

"Those two," Polly said. "They're always sparring. Peas in a pod."

The twins, sensing someone's presence, stopped and walked towards them, breathless. They looked at Polly in confusion, clearly wondering who their new guest was.

"I know, it's not often that we get visitors," Polly said, "but this one is special. Caitlin is her name. Please make her feel welcome. She saved me from some miscreants in Venice. We owe her one. Well, *I* owe her one, anyway."

"Have you cleared it with Aiden?" Tyler asked.

Polly paused, and Caitlin's stomach tightened. She hoped that she wasn't intruding.

"Not yet," Polly said. "He's off somewhere. But I'm sure he'll be agreeable. How could he not? She's darling. We could use someone like her. Not to mention, the room next to mine is empty."

"I'm Taylor," she said, reaching out her hand with a warm, friendly smile.

Caitlin was tempted to say, *I know.*

Instead, she merely reached out and took her hand.

Taylor's hand, cold and firm, felt very real, and helped bring her back to reality.

"A pleasure to meet you," Caitlin said.

"And what have we here?" Taylor asked, as she reached down and petted a willing Rose. "My, she's adorable."

"I'm Tyler," he said, elbowing his way in, and grinning down at Caitlin. As she shook his hand, she could feel his attraction to her, and she remembered the first time they'd met, in Pollepel. Some things never changed.

Tyler suddenly screamed and jumped.

Taylor stood behind him, grinning, having just whacked him hard with her wooden sword in the back of the leg. "Stop idling around," she said. "We have a dance to get ready for."

Tyler jumped back into the fight, swinging wildly at her, she parrying blow for blow.

Polly continued down the corridor, and Caitlin followed.

"This is where we live and train," Polly said. "We've been here for hundreds of years. I can't envision us ever leaving this place, unless there were a really good reason."

Caitlin thought of the future, and for a moment, debated telling Polly that she would, indeed, one day leave this place. But she realized that if she did, Polly would think she was totally crazy. Besides, why disappoint her?

Still, it was weird, knowing what Polly's future would be, when Polly herself didn't even know. It made Caitlin realize that we all feel so certain things will never change, but eventually, all of our plans never quite end up exactly how we thought.

"It's usually packed in here," Polly said, as they continued down a corridor. "But not today. Most of us are sleeping. Getting ready for the big night."

Caitlin looked over the place, and thought of the twins, and wondered about the other coven members. Was there anyone else she'd know? Her heart beat faster, as she suddenly remembered: Blake. She was almost afraid to ask.

"Among your coven members, is there somebody here named Blake?"

"No Blake here," Polly said. "Why?"

Caitlin breathed a sigh of relief. She was on edge enough as it was just looking for Caleb. Having Blake there now, too, would just be too much.

"No reason," she said, then quickly changed the subject. "So what is this Ball, exactly?"

Polly looked at her, eyes wide in excitement. "It's only the biggest night of the year. I've been waiting for ages. Everyone, and I mean *everyone*, will be there. Not just humans, but every vampire, too. Everyone has a date. Everyone looks stunning," she said, getting more excited as she went.

Caitlin thought. *Everyone.* She wondered if that meant Caleb.

"So, are there…vampires from all the covens?" Caitlin asked.

"Everyone who's anyone in the vampire world," Polly said. "Not just the surrounding covens—they come from all over Europe. It's the very best of high society. Not only that, it's also a masquerade. You would not believe it— there are the most elaborate costumes. You can't get in without a mask. And it goes on for hours. No one knows who's who. It's always someone different than you think."

"Are there parties here all the time?" Caitlin asked. "This whole city seems like it's drunk."

"You've really never been here, have you?" Polly shook her head in disbelief. "It's Carnival season. It's days and days of games, parties, drinking, gambling....That's why it's such a madhouse here. I mean, it's *always* a madhouse in Venice, but now, especially. Everyone's out in force. The finest costumes from all of Europe, all in one place. It's like a huge party, and it never ends. You came at the perfect time! And very convenient for vampires, I might add: with everyone in costumes, no one thinks twice about whether someone is human."

Polly opened an arched, oak door, and entered a small room, leaving the door open. Caitlin followed tentatively, with Rose.

This was clearly Polly's bedroom. The simple stone room had a large window in it, looking out at the trees, and Polly had a big, comfortable straw bed, covered in a pink linen and in what looked like straw teddy bears. Polly blushed at the site, and quickly shoved them under her pillow.

There were clothes strewn all over the floor, and all over her wooden dresser. Polly quickly tried to tidy the place.

"Sorry," she said, "my room is such a mess. I wasn't expecting any guests. Aiden would kill me if he saw it like this. But what does he expect? Tonight's the big dance. And I still have absolutely no idea what I'm wearing," she said, as she hurried through the room, trying to make sense of the chaos.

Caitlin saw several elaborate dresses along the wall, and several intricate masks. She was amazed by their craftsmanship. They looked like works of art. Some had long, curved noses, while others were small, no more than just an eye mask. There were gold masks and silver masks, some simple, and others elaborately adorned. Some were sinister, some jovial; some had feathers, others were plain. It was quite a collection.

Caitlin, fascinated, made her way over to the wall, and reached up and touched one.

"Go ahead, try it on," Polly said. "It's fun. You can be anyone you want. And you can switch every night. That's what Venice is about."

Caitlin gingerly removed a mask. It was the most unusual of them all. It was ornate, with a Persian or Indian influence, and its colors were copper, gold, and a burnt orange. A pattern of flowers was carved over the forehead and down between the eyes, giving it a regal quality.

Caitlin reached up and gently put it on her face. She walked over to the mirror, and then remembered. No reflection.

"I know, it sucks, doesn't it?" Polly asked. "I can never tell what I look like. It's *so* frustrating. I don't know why I even keep a mirror. I guess I'm hoping one day it will work. In the meantime, you just have to learn to go by what other people say."

Caitlin couldn't see what she looked like, but she felt different just wearing it. She felt like she'd stepped into someone else's shoes, like she had a license to be anyone. It felt liberating.

"It suits you well," Polly said. "You can wear it tonight."

A pang of fear raced through Caitlin.

"Tonight?" she asked, her voice nearly cracking.

"You're coming, aren't you?" Polly said, then grabbed her wrist. "Oh, you *have* to come. You just *have* to. How could you possibly miss it? *Please.* I could use the backup. Everyone else here is so boring, or they have dates. I'd love to have you with me. The best boys, the *very* best boys will be there, and it helps to have support. It will be so fun. Please, *please,*" Polly said, grabbing her arm.

Caitlin thought. The last thing on her mind right now was going to a dance, or looking for boys. All that mattered to her was Caleb, and she simply could not allow herself to rest, or enjoy herself, until she found him.

She slowly removed the mask and handed it to Polly.

"I'm sorry, Polly," she said. "I don't want to disappoint you. But I can't go. I really need to focus on finding someone."

"That guy you asked about? Caleb?" Polly asked. "Well, if so, then you *need* to go. I'm *sure* he'll be there. If he's one of us, that's where he'll be. You *have* to go. For your own sake."

Caitlin thought about it, and as she did, she realized it made sense. If Polly was right, if this ball was really such a big affair, maybe he *would* be there. Besides, she had no other leads, no other ideas for where to search for him. Perhaps she should go.

But another worry struck her: she had nothing to wear. She was never good at going to dances; she always got so nervous leading up to them. And this sounded like the biggest, most formal dance yet. Plus, she wasn't even a good dancer in the 21st century—how could she possibly dance well in the 18th? She would just look clumsy, conspicuous, stupid.

"Don't worry, the dances are easy," Polly said, annoyingly reading Caitlin's mind again. "I'll teach you, I promise. Just grab the wrist of the person next to you, and they lead you along. Everyone's so drunk anyway, I promise no one will notice."

"Drunk?" Caitlin asked. "Do they let girls our age drink? Isn't there, like, an age limit?"

For a brief moment, Caitlin worried about getting in, about having I.D.

Polly laughed aloud. "Are you kidding? This is Venice. No one cares. Toddlers can drink if they want to."

"But I've nothing to wear," Caitlin protested.

Polly's eyes lit up. "Oh, but you do," she said. "Have you not seen this room? I have enough gowns here to last me for fifteen balls. And we look to be the same size. *Please*, try one on. Let's have fun! It's almost the 19th century, after all! When else will we get a chance to live like this!?"

Caitlin thought. She certainly had a point. If not now, when? And she'd always wanted to try on one of those elaborate gowns.

Not to mention, if Caleb *was* there, what better way to meet him again than in a beautiful, elaborate gown?

The more Caitlin thought about it, the more she liked the idea.

Maybe going to the ball would be just the thing she needed.

CHAPTER NINE

Kyle, flying over the hillsides of Umbria, dove in lower as he circled the small, medieval town of Assisi. He got a good glimpse of its medieval walls, of the huge church that dominated the village. In the sunset light, villagers were spread out below, lighting torches, herding their cattle, bringing their chickens and sheep inside. Everyone was hurrying to and fro, as if to prepare: this seemed like a town that feared the night.

Kyle smiled. He would give them a whole new reason to.

There were few things that Kyle enjoyed more than striking panic and fear into the hearts of commoners, in giving them new nightmares to dwell on for the rest of their lives. He hated this type of simple folk. They had persecuted his kind for as long as he could remember, and Kyle felt that it was long past due that they got a good thrashing themselves. Whenever he found the opportunity, he relished the chance.

Kyle dove lower, aiming right for the town square, not far from the church, hoping that his sudden and dramatic landing would stir up some activity, perhaps even flesh Caitlin out. If that despicable little girl was here, he wanted to waste no time in catching her. He was already itching to go back to the 21st century, to continuing his war, and to be done with this petty little distraction.

Of course, he had the Grand Council to answer to, and they wanted her alive. It was an annoyance, but a necessary one. He could play along, could capture her for now, just to appease them. But he would personally escort her back, and he would not leave until he personally watched her tortured and killed. In fact, he would quite enjoy that. But this time, he would leave nothing to chance. If they delayed, he would finish her off himself—with their approval or not.

As Kyle landed with a flurry in the town square, his black wings spread wide, sending a gust of wind that sent dogs yelping and chickens flying, villagers in every direction erupted into a scream. Old ladies crossed themselves, and young boys fled for their lives. It was as if a bomb had landed.

A few of the more courageous ones grabbed farming instruments and bore down on him.

Kyle smiled. He loved these types. If they were his kind, he might even befriend them.

Kyle easily ducked as one of them swung his hoe clumsily at his head; then he reached up and, in one simple move, tore his head clean off his body.

Kyle delighted at the site of the gushing blood. He bent over and sank his teeth into what was left of the man's throat, and drank greedily. He felt the blood rushing through his veins with a thrill. It was just the afternoon snack he needed.

The other two villagers, upon seeing this, literally froze in their tracks with fear, dropping their instruments. So much the easier for Kyle.

Kyle walked up and grabbed each by his throat, lifting them cleanly off the ground, and smashed them into each other with such force that he killed them on the spot.

Screams rang through the courtyard and the church bells tolled, as everyone fled to their homes, locking the doors and shuttering their windows.

A mob of a dozen men came running over the hilltop, all carrying farming instruments, screaming and charging right for Kyle. Kyle smiled. They still had not learned their lesson.

Kyle didn't wait. He charged them himself, meeting them halfway, and as they swung at him, he suddenly leapt over the entire group, and landed behind them. Before they could react, he grabbed the closest one by the back of his head, grabbing his hair and lifting him off the ground. He swung him like a rag doll, and then threw him into the crowd. They went down like dominoes.

Before they could regain their feet, Kyle grabbed one of their sickles, and swung wildly. Using his vampire lightning speed, he attacked the flustered men as if they were a bale of hay. He chopped them to pieces.

Within moments, all of them were dead.

The village square now a blood-soaked battleground, Kyle stepped over the mangled bodies, and walked casually towards the church. As he did, he watched the doors get slammed and bolted. He smiled. He wondered why people always thought that bolting doors would make any difference.

Kyle leaned back and kicked in the huge church doors, knocking them off their hinges.

He strutted into the ancient church of Assisi, and headed right down the aisle. As he did, he tore up pew after pew, hurling them across the room, up high, into the windows, shattering the ancient stained-glass. He reached up and grabbed a huge candelabra and snapped it off its rope, and swung it over his head. When he let go, it went flying through the church, smashing the stained-glass windows on the far wall.

Kyle surveyed the destruction. It was beautiful. There were few things he enjoyed more than smashing up a church.

He sensed Caitlin's presence. He followed his senses, and they led him down a corridor, down a flight of steps, and into the lower levels of the church. As he turned the final corner, he was surprised by what he saw.

Standing there was a small, silver haired priest, staring back at him. Kyle sensed immediately that this man was of his race. It surprised him to see him in a priest's garb. What a sacrilege for his race.

"The girl you seek is long gone," the priest said, unafraid. He stared at Kyle with courage, unwavering.

"And you'll never find her," he said.

Kyle smiled.

"Is that right?" he said.

Kyle took several steps towards him, but the man showed no sign of backing down. He was far braver—or dumber—than Kyle thought.

"You can overpower me," the priest said, "but God overpowers you. You can kill me on this day, but God will surely kill you on another, and I will be avenged. Death holds no fear for me."

"Who said anything about killing you?" Kyle asked, as he got closer. "That would be too kind. I think, instead, I'll torture you slowly."

"That makes little difference to me," the man said. "No matter what you do, you will never find her."

Kyle bore down on the man, just feet away, and leapt at him.

But the man surprised him. At the last second, the man reached back and threw a handful of holy ash right into Kyle's eyes.

Kyle fell to the ground, stunned, his eyes burning. Holy ash. A sneaky trick. It hurt like hell; he hadn't had it in his eyes for centuries.

"I renounce you in the name of Satan," the man said. "Let this holy ash destroy you, and let it send you back to the place from which you came."

He threw down handful after handful of ash onto Kyle's head.

But Kyle suddenly regained his strength and charged the man, tackling him hard, sending him to the ground.

On top of him, Kyle grabbed his throat, and squeezed.

The man stared back with eyes opened wide, clearly in shock.

"Stupid man," Kyle spat. "Holy ash can only kill the weak of our race. I developed immunity hundreds of years ago."

The man struggled for breath, as Kyle squeezed.

Kyle grinned wider.

"And now, it's my turn," Kyle said. "You and I are going to get to know each other. Very, very well."

CHAPTER TEN

As Caitlin, all dressed up in an elaborate gown, followed Polly through the door, she had to stop herself at the last second from stepping right into the water. She still couldn't get over the fact that doors opened right onto the water, that one could step into the water as easily as one would step onto a sidewalk elsewhere.

As Caitlin stood there, at the water's edge, in the fading sunset, she looked down at the rippling water, and was finally able to see her reflection.

"Look!" Caitlin said in amazement, grabbing Polly's arm, in shock that she could actually see herself.

"I know," Polly said. "We use it all the time. It's our only way of seeing ourselves. It's not exactly a mirror, but it has to do."

Caitlin was startled at how she looked. She wore a huge gown, yellow, gold and white, festive and multi-layered, with floral designs all over it. Her hair had been braided by Polly, and Caitlin completed her costume with her Venetian mask. She especially liked the mask. Behind this mask, she could have been anyone. With it on, she seemed so mysterious, so regal, even a bit dangerous.

Caitlin looked up and saw that all around her, Polly's coven members, dozens of them, were at the water's edge, preparing to board their gondolas. She was impressed by how they looked: they were all so dressed up, in gowns and masks of every color and fabric and style. They had spent all afternoon preparing, and they took it seriously. Their formality was so different from what Caitlin was used to. In a weird way, it was refreshing. They were all so elegant, so refined. Caitlin thought back to what it was like going out for the night in the 21st century. She would spend maybe 10 minutes getting ready, maybe throw on jeans and a turtleneck. That all seemed so boring, so commonplace, next to this. The people in this century seemed to really embrace living life to the fullest.

It was a bit of a challenge for Caitlin to get into the narrow, rocking gondola in her huge gown. Tyler, a boat over, saw her struggling, and hurried over and held out his hand for her.

"Thanks," she said, taking it.

She took two steps into the rickety boat, swayed and then balanced yourself, as the boat rocked all over the place. She managed to quickly sit and tuck her gown in, right before it draped into the water.

Rose whined, looking on from the water's edge, clearly wanting to come.

"Sorry, Rose," Caitlin said. "Not this time. Don't worry, I'll be back soon."

Rose kept whining, wanting to be by her side, and Caitlin felt bad. But at the same time, she was happy at the thought of Rose on this island, safe and secure.

All around them, coven members were boarding their gondolas. There was a small fleet of about a dozen gondolas, with two people in each, one sitting down low, and the other standing and rowing. Caitlin recognized many of them: Taylor and Tyler, Cain and Barbara, Patrick, Madeline, Harrison...Polly had introduced her to all of them again throughout the day. It was so weird for her to be introduced to all these people she already knew. But she went along with it, and everything had gone smoothly. Even Cain was nice to her this time.

They all welcomed her as if she'd been there forever, and once again, she felt at home with them. She was starting to feel as if everything she'd lost on Pollepel was slowly being restored to her. Once again, she was slowly beginning to feel like she was home. But she was scared of the feeling, too: it seemed like every time she settled into a place, something ended up happening to uproot her.

The boats pushed off, cutting their way through the clear blue water, lit up in the twilight by the rising full moon. The water was rougher now, at night, than it had been earlier, and her boat bobbed up and down. But it was a peaceful, repetitive motion, and it set her at ease, as did the sound of the waves lapping against it. Caitlin leaned back and closed her eyes, feeling the salt air on her face, and breathed deeply. It was a warm night, and she felt completely relaxed.

She heard a voice break out into song, and opened her eyes and looked over. One of her coven members, in a neighboring boat, was singing as he rowed. It was in a language she did not understand, and he sung in a deep, melodic voice. It was slow, sad song, which merged with the sounds of the lapping waves and the occasional bird crying overhead.

Caitlin closed her eyes again, and allowed herself to relax. Once again, she felt at home, a sense of ease in the world. She allowed her mind to wander, and to think of the night to come.

Despite all the stark cultural differences, despite being dressed in a costume and mask and being in the year 1790 and heading to a ball, Caitlin felt that things weren't really all that different than they might be back home. She almost felt as if she could be going out with friends on a Saturday night, heading to a dance. The exteriors were very different, but ultimately, deep down, it was the same thing. Going out for the night with friends. Hoping to have a good time. Hoping to meet someone. It was amazing to her how some things never changed.

In Caitlin's case, the only thing on her mind was Caleb. She felt her heart pounding with excitement with every row the boat took, hoping that it took her one step closer to meeting him. She felt with her whole heart that she would see him at the dance tonight. She *willed* it to be the case. She prayed, she really prayed, that he was alive, that he had survived the trip. That he would be there. It seemed like the best chance she had.

If he wasn't here, if he hadn't made it, she would be crushed. And if he was there… She didn't even know where to begin. She tried to imagine the moment. Seeing him again for the first time. She prayed that he would recognize her, that their love would make it possible. That the second their eyes locked, he would embrace her, would remember everything. He would tell her how he had been searching for her, too, and how grateful he was to have her back. He would thank her for reviving him. He would tell her how happy he was that they could live together now, free from any harm.

Caitlin's heart swelled as she thought of it. It was a chance to start clean with Caleb, and it was a chance to meet him for the first time all over again. In a way, it would be like a first date. And maybe there would be a first dance. And a first kiss.

And then…just maybe, they could get married this time. And have a child once again.

*

It was dark by the time they arrived in Venice, and as they rounded a bend and approached the city, Caitlin was struck by its beauty at night. The city was lit up, candles in every window, and torches on every boat. The water, filled with boats, was even more crowded than before, lit with the reflection of thousands of torches from hundreds of ships gliding through the night. If anything, the city look even more festive during the night than it had during the day. Caitlin was shocked at how much they managed to achieve without electricity.

And, to Caitlin's surprise, it was even more crowded. Even from this distance, she could hear the laughing, the singing, and most of all, the music. In every direction, on every corner, in every square, even in the boats, people were playing music, strumming on lutes, harps, guitars...It was as if they were entering one huge party.

People were also openly drinking everywhere, and laughter filled the air. It soared above the noise, as if everyone seemed to be in a fit of hysterics over something.

Caitlin looked forward to re-entering the city, especially, this time, with all of her newfound friends in tow, but she was still a bit intimidated by the maze of streets, and by the crowds. People were everywhere, and with everyone was in costume, it seemed far too easy to get separated and lost in the fray.

Their gondola headed under a bridge, and then pulled up to the dock. All of her coven members jumped out, securing their boats, and giving each other a hand.

Before Caitlin could even stand, Tyler had jumped out of his boat, run over to hers, and knelt down, offering her hand.

"Aren't you going to offer *me* a hand?" Polly asked, joking.

"She's the new girl," Tyler said. "She needs it."

Caitlin took his hand gladly, hoping that he didn't look too much into it, as she stepped out of the rocky boat; with one big step, he lifted her and she jumped onto shore. It was no easy feat, and she wondered how she'd ever get back into it.

Before Polly could get off, Patrick suddenly appeared, running over to her and holding out his hand.

"Can I help you, Polly?" he asked, hopefully. He stood there with his big grin, large ears, and shock of red hair, and looked exactly as Caitlin had remembered him on Pollepel.

"Thanks anyway," Polly said, "but I'll be OK."

Patrick turned away, crestfallen.

Caitlin marveled at the twists of fate. She remembered a time when Polly was desperate to court Patrick; now, the situation had clearly changed.

Caitlin felt happy to be on land, standing there with all of her new friends, ready to see the city at night for the first time. In her first trip here, she had felt so disoriented; now, she really felt ready to take it all in.

The group of them hurried off into the crowd, and Caitlin stuck close by Polly's side, careful not to lose her. It shouldn't be too hard, because Polly's bright pink and white dress—and matching mask—was hard to miss. Polly reached over and grabbed Caitlin's wrist, as they were jostled every which way through the crowd.

"Venice is unlike any place in the world," Polly said. "The city is in decline, but no one really cares. It's sinking, literally, into the water, but no one seems to care about that, either. They just want to have fun. People come here from all over the world to join in the party, and to shake their heads at our lifestyle." Polly shrugged. "We're far removed from it being on our island—but when we do come in, it's always a good time."

They all turned down a side street, and then into a large square, buildings facing it from every direction with elaborate, marble façades. It was beautiful, and the square was absolutely packed, aglow with torches.

Caitlin wondered if the crowds would ever die down, anywhere in this city.

The square was lined with cafés along one side, hundreds of people sitting at small tables, mostly in costume and wearing masks, sipping on cups of coffee, or drinking glasses of wine.

The clinking of dishes could be heard from far away. Dogs roamed amidst them, scavenging for scraps.

As they crossed to the other side of the square, Caitlin saw that it was lined with gambling booths: there were hundreds of small tables, hustlers behind them, moving small shells or offering various other ways for unsuspecting victims to gamble their money. Crowded around them were hundreds of people, betting away their money on sure losses.

There was a sudden eruption and shouting, as one of the tables was knocked over by an angry customer. He pounced on the hustler, and the two of them wrestled to the ground, punching and hitting each other, as a commotion broke out.

Caitlin felt a tug on her arm, and followed Polly as the group turned down another side street. This alleyway was narrow, barely big enough to fit a few people side-by-side, and it was darker than the others. As they walked, wooden shutters opened above them on all sides, and girls, not much older than Caitlin, stuck their heads out, smiling widely, and pulling their dresses low enough to reveal their breasts.

Caitlin was shocked.

"Want a good time?" one of them called out.

"Hey honey!" screamed another

"I'm for hire!" another screamed.

Caitlin felt bad that girls her age had to work that way, and she marveled at the injustice of the world. Some things never seemed to change.

They entered another square, and this one was filled with jugglers, fire eaters, and all sorts of games. The music here was even louder, as a whole band of performers strummed guitars, and a chorus of people sang along.

"Drink? Drink?"

A jug of wine was thrust under Caitlin's nose, as several vendors crowded around them, shoving it under their faces. She tried to push them away, but they kept getting closer. Finally, Polly reached over and shoved them hard, and they went away.

"It's the only way to handle them," Polly said.

Caitlin was taken aback by the roughness of this place. It seemed like complete mayhem.

As she headed deeper into yet another thick crowd, she began to feel claustrophobic. It was getting harder to move, as the crowd seemed to grow continually thicker, people pouring into the square from all directions. Worse, she was overwhelmed by the stench. It seemed no one bathed, and that the closest attempt was throwing on cheap perfume, which didn't even work.

Caitlin looked over and noticed Polly take out a small pouch from her pocket, and raise it to her nose.

"What's that?" Caitlin asked.

Polly looked over, and realize that Caitlin didn't have one, and reached into her pocket and handed her one. It felt funny in Caitlin's hand, like a small, silk bag of potpourri.

"Hold it to your nose," Polly instructed. "It helps."

Caitlin held it up, and it helped right away. Instead of the smell of the people, she inhaled the scent of roses and perfume.

"It's really impossible to get through Venice without it."

Caitlin surveyed the crowd, and saw the other coven members were holding them, too.

They finally exited onto a side street, and as they walked, the street ended in a footbridge. They had to ascend, up about 15 steps or so, then the bridge flattened out, over a canal of water. Caitlin looked left and right as they did, and saw the canal wind its way through the narrow side streets of Venice. Seeing water like that, right in the middle of the city, was really incredible. It was amazing to her that she couldn't have continued walking down this street without crossing a small bridge.

They came down the footbridge on the other end, and turned down another side street, and entered yet another square. The square was much more elegant than the others, lined with huge palaces, elaborate marble façades, arched doorways, and huge arched windows. Caitlin wondered if this was where royalty lived.

Just as she was about to ask Polly where they were, the group stopped in front of one of the more beautiful buildings, before an oak door. One of them reached up, grabbed the metal knocker, and slammed it with three short knocks that echoed throughout the plaza.

Within seconds, an elaborately dressed butler opened the door. He bowed his head and stepped aside.

"Just on time," he said with a smile.

*

Caitlin entered the huge palace, sticking close to Polly, and looked up at her surroundings in awe. It was unlike any place she had ever been. This huge, opulent palace had soaring ceilings, painted with frescoes and lined with fancy moldings. The walls were covered in oil paintings and enormous gold mirrors. A gigantic chandelier hung low, holding dozens of candles which lit up the room. Beneath Caitlin's feet was an intricate black-and-white tiled marble floor, so shiny that she could almost see her reflection in it. Before her was a wide marble staircase, winding to the left and to the right with an ornate railing, and lush red carpeting right down the middle.

The room was packed with people. It was a different sort of crowd than had filled the streets—here, the people seemed refined, elegant, and were clearly very, very rich. They were all dripping with jewelry—some of the most brilliant and opulent jewels Caitlin had ever seen. Their costumes were more fancy, more ornate, and everyone wore masks, some covered in jewels. The laughter in here was more subtle, and nearly everyone drank from a crystal glass. It felt like she was in an exclusive cocktail party inside a lavish museum. There were hundreds of people milling about, as far as her eye could see.

The room was also filled with music. In the corner of the room sat a string quartet, the mellow sounds of the violin and cello echoing off the high walls. Caitlin wondered who lived here. Was it some sort of government palace? Or was it a private residence?

"It's the Doge's Palace," Polly said, answering her thoughts, as she tugged on her arm, leading her through the crowd. "He's the elected ruler of the humans. The palace is used for parties by the richest family in Venice. They've ruled this town for hundreds of years."

"How did they get so rich?" Caitlin asked.

"Salt."

"Salt?" Caitlin asked, thinking she'd misheard.

"It used to be a precious commodity. There was a time when no one in Europe could get it. And Venice had it in troves. Haven't you seen the water? Smelled the air? It's packed with salt. That's why all the buildings are rotting. The salt water's corroding their foundations.

"When the first Venetians came here, they quickly realized they were sitting on a gold mine. All they had to do was extract salt from the water. It was like minting money, and they created more wealth than you or I could ever imagine."

They continued weaving through more of the crowd.

"But it's a dying family now," Polly continued. "Their empire is dwindling. The descendants now are nothing like their ancestors. But some of them are kind of cute. I've got my eye on one in particular. Robert. The grandson. He's about our age, and he's never been turned. He's fabulous," she said, her eyes lighting up. "He wears the most outrageous outfits. I think he likes me, too. I'm hoping he'll ask me to dance tonight. Every time I see him, he's spending money in the most ridiculous, lavish way."

They finally reached the far end of the room and Polly opened a grand door, and as she did, Caitlin's jaw dropped.

"Like hiring Mozart," Polly added.

There, on the far side of the room, seated at the end of an immense banquet table, sat Wolfgang Amadeus Mozart.

Wearing a white wig, dressed in an elaborate costume, he was the only one in the room without a mask—and the only one who didn't need one. His personality was more than enough. Short, pudgy and very pale, he sat behind a harpsichord, drinking with one hand and playing with the other. When he set down the goblet, he broke into wild laughter, and continued playing with both hands.

For all his levity, his music was intense, spiritual. It was unlike anything Caitlin had ever heard. She had, in fact, never heard a harpsichord in her life. It had a tin, metallic sound, and it was not very loud—yet it really resonated in its own way. His playing was fun, upbeat, playful. Much like the man himself. But still, there was an undercurrent to it, something so profound.

The table already sat about a hundred, and was half full with humans. There remained about fifty empty chairs, and Caitlin found herself led to the table with her coven members. They all sat together, completing the table, and the other diners all raised a glass and cheered as they did. Caitlin's group raised their glasses back, and as Caitlin picked hers up, she saw that it was already conveniently filled with a red liquid.

Caitlin sat in the lush, red velvet armchair, sinking into it, propping her elbows on its huge arms, and examined her glass. It was fine crystal, the red liquid illuminated by the huge candelabra on the table. She had a feeling she knew what it was, and as she drank, she realized she was right: blood. It coursed through her veins with a rush, energizing her, and she realized there was something else mixed in, too—some kind of alcohol. Caitlin felt it go right to her head, and felt a bit dizzy. She also felt relaxed. She realized how on-edge she'd been since she'd arrived.

Elegant china was set before her, on which was a small piece of raw meat. Similar plates were being placed before all of her coven members. The fleet of waiters disappeared, and before they'd even left, another fleet arrived, setting down all sorts of delicacies and meats on the table. In the center sat a huge stuffed pig, an apple in its mouth.

There was more food on this table than Caitlin had ever seen, and every second it seemed another servant brought out a new dish. This was in addition to the dozens of servers who circled around them, constantly refilling everyone's glasses. They filled Caitlin's side of the table with the dark liquid, and filled all the others with what looked like champagne.

Caitlin wanted to ask Polly what this was all about, why they were here, whose house this was, but she was too mesmerized by Mozart. Caitlin didn't understand classical music, and didn't know how to appreciate it, but even so, it was obvious, even to a layperson, that he played with a skill and passion unlike anything anyone in the room had ever known. The man was on fire. Music seemed to stream right from his fingertips, completing the festive atmosphere. Equally amazingly, he laughed and drank as he played without even missing a note.

All of the people around the table were drinking and laughing. The doors to the huge room were left wide open, and other people continually streamed in and out, the party extending itself into the room, and spreading out all around them. It was less of a formal dining room than it was a dining table set in the

145

midst of a cocktail party. Caitlin could hardly believe the lavishness of this place.

"What is all this?" Caitlin finally asked Polly. "Why are we here? Whose place is this? I thought we were going to a ball?"

Polly had a piece of raw meat in her mouth, sucking the blood from it, savoring every ounce. She finally put it down, looking refreshed, and wiped her mouth and looked over at Caitlin.

"This is Venice, my dear," she said. "Nothing ever starts on time. And everything is always preceded by something else. We would never jump right into a ball. Before that is dinner; and before that, music; and before that, drinking; and before that, games. Life here is not about merely going to an event and leaving. It is about making an event last all night long."

Caitlin could already tell that that was the case. As she looked up, she saw a bunch of circus performers approach the far side of the table, rolling carts with all sorts of balls on them. Another cart rolled up with shells on them. As the table watched, they shuffled the shells in every direction.

"That one!" someone yelled, reaching out and pointing a finger at a shell.

It was a heavy woman, covered in too much makeup, sitting on a man's lap, and as she screamed, she reached over and pushed a huge pile of gold coins into the center of the table.

"No, no, that one!" screamed someone else, pushing their own pile of coins.

After a dramatic pause, the performer lifted the shell and revealed the empty one. The table erupted into a roar of delight.

The woman who had guessed correctly gathered her coins, plus others, and leaned over and kissed the man she was with.

Caitlin looked around the table, and noticed that many women were sitting on men's laps, and that some were kissing passionately, in full view of the others. No one seemed to care.

"Don't you think he's fabulous?" Polly asked.

Caitlin followed her gaze to the head of the table. Seated there was an arrogant looking fellow, maybe 18, with striking features. He had dark brown hair, brown eyes, was clean shaven, and looked like he'd been pampered his entire life.

"That's him," Polly continued, "Robert."

Polly was right: he was dressed fabulously, and he was very attractive. But he was not Caitlin's type at all. He seemed so full of himself. He wore his gold mask pulled back, sitting on his forehead, and held a ruby-encrusted goblet. Several attractive woman stood behind him, one with a hand on his shoulder.

He suddenly looked right at Caitlin, raised his glass, and nodded.

"Oh my God, did you see that?" Polly asked. "He looked right at us! Did you see!? I think he was looking at me! I really hope we dance tonight."

Caitlin felt a twinge of nervousness in her stomach. She knew, without a doubt, that Robert had been looking at her, not at Polly. She was suddenly afraid that he liked her, and, if so, that Polly would hate her for it. She always seemed to end up in these situations.

Caitlin settled into her overstuffed chair, realizing she was in for a long night. On the one hand, it was fun. But on the other hand, it was too much. Over the top. Decadent. There was just too much of everything—too much food, too much wine, too many games, too many people. It seemed never ending.

All she wanted was to see Caleb. She desperately missed him, now more than ever, with every pore of her body. She had imagined herself coming out tonight, walking right into the ball, and finding him right away. These drinks, these games, this dinner—it all felt like a distraction. It was prolonging her from seeing him. She started to grow impatient.

"So when does the dance start?" Caitlin asked.

"Oh, never before midnight," Polly said casually, as she took another sip of her wine.

Midnight, Caitlin thought. She looked across the room, at a huge grandfather clock, and saw that it had just struck nine.

She was in for a long night, indeed.

*

Caitlin was slumped in her chair, feeling lightheaded from the endless glasses of wine, from the nonstop, hysterical laughter from every direction, from dish after dish landing in front of her. It was a hedonistic feast unlike anything she had ever experienced. She could hardly believe that this was all just the *warm up* to the night.

She observed everything carefully, so curious about how people acted and what they talked about, in 1790. She concluded that a dinner party was a very, very different experience. Everyone here really engaged each other, valued each other's presence, was engrossed in conversation. No one was on cell phones; no one was texting; no one was checking their voicemails or Facebook page. No telephones rang; no electronics buzzed. And soft candlelight took the place of electricity. It was all so much more relaxed, more slow-paced, more civil. No one was in a rush; everyone seemed to have all the time in the world. Maybe that was what happened, she figured, when you took technology away.

And yet, it was not unsophisticated: the China, the crystal, the silverware, the elaborate dress, the gourmet meal, the vintage wines...It could have been like something out of a gourmet restaurant of the 21st century.

At the same time, they didn't seem to have a great regard for their health. Had they ever heard of cholesterol? They drank and ate as if there were no consequences, as if they would all drop dead tomorrow. And she assumed that most of these people had never seen a gym—or even knew what that was. It was baffling.

As Caitlin slumped further, absolutely stuffed, her eyes began to close—and suddenly, the clock rang out.

Everyone stood, and Caitlin realized the large clock had struck midnight.

As everyone got up, a set of double doors opened on the far side of the room, leading to a ballroom.

Caitlin got up with the others, Polly taking her arm excitedly, and they all hurried, with the crowd, towards the ballroom. More and more people flowed in from all the rooms, and within moments, the massive room was completely filled.

This huge room was much like the others: it boasted a black and white tiled marble floor, a massive fireplace, chandeliers filled with burning candles and gold mirrors on every wall, reflecting the light, making this immense room seem even bigger than it was. Hundreds of people were already in it, and more and more poured through the doors. The room was so wide, Caitlin could hardly see the other end from where she stood. She craned her neck, searching for Caleb, but it was no use. There was a sea of bodies, and, besides, they were all wearing masks.

Caitlin was nervous as the music began. Mozart sat at the far end of the room, on a small dais, and began playing the harpsichord; as he did, cellists and violinists joined in. It was an upbeat, formal waltz.

Everyone in the room knew what to do. Everyone, that is, but Caitlin. She stood to the side, feeling like an idiot, as everyone lined up perfectly on either side. She looked for Polly, nearly losing her amidst the throng, and hurried to her side.

"Don't worry, it's an easy dance," Polly said. "They always start with easy ones."

The entire room moved in perfect synchronicity, holding their arms out to the sides, taking one step forward then two steps back, half turning to the right than half turning to the left. Caitlin tried to follow, and as she did, she'd never felt so clumsy. She'd never been a good dancer, and she had no idea what kind of dance this was. Her one saving grace was that the tempo was slow enough for her to catch up with the others.

Caitlin again scanned the crowd, hoping for a glimpse of Caleb. But with all the costumes and masks, it was impossible to even tell who was really male or female. Occasionally, long hair sprawled out the back, and that made it easy, but some women wore their hair tucked in, covered up by a high collar, and dressed in men's clothing. And some men, Caitlin noticed, strangely enough, dressed in gowns; she could only tell they were men by the muscles in their calves. She had never imagined that there would be any cross-dressing in this century. Was there anything off-limits?

Caitlin was just beginning to get the hang of the song, when suddenly the music stopped. Mozart, with a loud laugh, suddenly started a new one, this one with a much faster tempo.

A new dance began. A set of four lines formed on opposite sides of the room, and the room paired off, grabbed each other, and waltzed in wide circles throughout the room.

"My God, there he is," Polly said, watching Robert dance across the room with a buxom blonde. Caitlin looked, but couldn't see what she saw in him.

Patrick came hurrying over to Polly, pulled back his mask, and smiled. He held out a hand.

"A dance?" he asked, hopefully.

He blocked Polly's view of Robert, and she craned her neck, annoyed.

"Maybe later," Polly said.

His smile dropped, as he slinked away.

"I have to try to get a dance with him," she said, and headed off into the crowd for Robert.

Caitlin stood there, feeling more alone than ever, and nervously scanned the faces again. This was not going as she had imagined at all. A blur of masks passed in front of her, one after the other. How could she possibly hope to find Caleb? As she tried to picture his face, it became harder and harder. She began to wonder if she ever even knew him at all. She felt a pit in her stomach, as she began to despair that he had never even survived the trip.

Caitlin tried to center herself, to use her senses. She closed her eyes and breathed deep, trying to shut out all the music, and noise, and movement. As she felt herself getting jostled, she tried to ignore it, to focus on Caleb. She took a deep breath, hoping she could somehow sense his presence. Deep down, she felt she would just *know* if he were in the same room.

"Caitlin?" suddenly came a man's voice.

Caitlin opened her eyes excitedly, her heart soaring.

Before her stood a man with elaborate green mask, and he broke into a smile. Had it worked?

Caitlin broke into a smile herself, hoping.

But when the man threw back the mask, Caitlin's heart broke.

Infuriatingly, it was Tyler.

The same old Tyler. After all these centuries, still trying to pick her up. "May I have this dance?" he asked.

Caitlin was annoyed. He had ruined her moment.

"No," she snapped, and turned away.

She saw his face fall in disappointment as he walked away.

She suddenly felt bad. She shouldn't have been so harsh with him. He certainly didn't deserve that; after all, he only asked her to dance, and it wasn't his fault. But he had caught her at the wrong moment. And now she felt even worse.

As Caitlin scanned the room, she began to despair. She didn't see how she could ever find

Caleb in this place. And clearly, her senses weren't helping her. There was too much going on, too much getting in the way of her focusing.

The music changed again, and the room transitioned into a new dance, one in which couples danced with each other, then switched off, each person dancing with someone new every few steps. As Caitlin watched it, she realized that was what she needed to find him. She had to join in, to sweep the entire room, to dance with as many people as she could. Just standing there was doing her no good. She needed to hold hands with as many people as she could. She knew, she just *knew*, that if her hands actually touched Caleb's, there was no way, *there was no possible way*, that she could not know.

Determined, Caitlin hurried out onto the floor with a new passion, grabbing the hands of the nearest partner, following the three-step dance clumsily, then switching off when everyone else did, and grabbing the hands of another.

The hands she grabbed were sweaty, and she could smell the alcohol coming out of their masks.

She danced and danced, finally getting the hang of it, switching off to so many people so quickly, that finally the room began to blur. At one point, she didn't even know if she had danced with a woman by accident. Everyone just kept switching off, faster and faster, as the music picked up. She danced from one side of the room to the other—again and again and again.

Always, it was a new hand. A new shoulder. A new spin, a new partner. Short ones and tall ones and skinny ones and fat ones. Each new person had an even more elaborate mask; some were funny and made her laugh, while others were sinister.

But still, no Caleb.

Finally, the music stopped. Caitlin, exhausted physically and emotionally, stopped to rest in a corner of the room. As everyone took a breath, she pulled back her mask and wiped the sweat from her forehead, breathing hard, as it was getting hot in here.

"May I request the pleasure of a dance?" came a voice.

Caitlin spun, hoping.

But it was not Caleb—she knew that already from the voice.

No, it was Robert. The Duke.

He was the *last* person she wanted to dance with. Not only because he was arrogant, but more importantly, because Polly liked him.

He stood there, facing her, cheeks red from too much wine, and with a ridiculous white feather protruding from the back of mask, climbing several feet into the air.

This time she would be more tactful.

"I'm sorry," she said, "but I'm taking a break."

His face reddened. "How dare you! Would you really dare to turn down a dance with me? Don't you know who I am? After all, you are just a commoner. You'd be well advised to accept my offer—while it lasts."

Despite herself, Caitlin broke into a laugh. It made her realize the stark difference between the 21st and 18th centuries, the class lines that still existed. This man needed a good dose of her time. Now she was mad.

"I wouldn't dance with you if you paid me," she said coldly.

The man's face scrunched up in indignation. He stormed off, stomping his feet. He had probably never been spoken to that way in his life.

Good, Caitlin thought. *It was past time that he had.*

Caitlin needed some air. It was so stuffy in here; not a single window was open, and the hundreds of moving bodies created a tremendous heat.

She began to cross the dance floor, and as she did, a new song started up, a slower, more romantic one. Partners again began pairing off. Caitlin tried to ignore them, to brush past them, but it was another switching song, and partners didn't ask. People grabbed whoever was on the floor, danced with them for several steps, and let them go, and Caitlin felt herself being grabbed and spun. There was simply no way around it.

She gave in, deciding that she would just dance her way across the room one last time, and then head for the exit. She switched from one partner to another, grabbing hands and letting go.

And then, it happened. As her hands touched those of her final partner, an electric shock ran through her body.

His hands, his energy. She felt it from her head down to her toes.

She looked up at him carefully. He wore a mask, a proud, golden mask of royalty, and she couldn't see his eyes. But her body told her.

She became breathless. The entire room stopped around here.

It had to be Caleb.

But as she opened her mouth to speak, a random dancer pulled her away, grabbed her and spun her in the other direction. At the same time, another dancer grabbed him away, and spun him in the other direction.

Caitlin tried to yank herself away, but he was too heavy and strong. By the time she managed to disengage, she was already halfway across the room, looking desperately for Caleb. She scoured every which way, looking for that golden mask, but he seemed to be gone, lost in the sea of bodies.

Frantic, Caitlin hurried through the room, shoving anyone in her way, absolutely determined to find him.

She did it again and again, crisscrossing the entire room, from one exit to the other.

Finally, after almost an hour, she was exhausted. He was nowhere to be found. If it had been him, he was gone.

Or had she imagined the whole thing?

Caitlin bent over, removed her mask, and breathed. She couldn't stand it. It was too much.

She ran out the nearest door and then kept running, through the lobby, and through another door.

Finally, she was outside, on the square, gulping in the fresh air. She removed her mask and felt overwhelmed with emotion.

She cried and cried and cried.

*

A bell tolled, and Caitlin looked up at the giant clock tower, on the opposite side of the square, and saw that it was four A.M. She couldn't believe how late she'd been out. If she had been home, in modern times, and it had been a school night, her mom would've killed her. Here, no one cared. There had been many teenage girls in that room, and there were still many of them hanging out here in the square, at four in the morning.

Caitlin was exhausted. She just wanted to go home, to go back to Polly's Island, and crash. She needed to sleep, to clear her head, to formulate a plan for finding Caleb—if he was even alive. She had been foolish, she realized now, to expect to find him in that ball. Even if that had been him, it clearly he was now gone for good.

She needed to go back in there, find Polly, and ask her if she was ready to go. She hoped that she was. The last thing she wanted was to wait here for hours more until Polly was ready to leave. And she didn't exactly have another way of getting back to the island—or any place else to go.

Caitlin went back inside the ballroom, and was a bit relieved to see that it was already petering out. It was half as crowded as it had been, and people were leaving by the minute.

Caitlin found Polly, luckily, and was concerned to see her crying. She hurried up to her.

"What's wrong?" she asked. "What happened?"

"Robert," Polly said. "I asked him to dance. At first, he said no. Then, he changed his mind, and danced with me, but it was like he didn't really want to dance. He was dancing too fast, like he was rushing to get through it, and jerking me around. He made me trip. He said I was a clumsy dancer. He made fun of me and people were laughing. I'm so embarrassed," she said, crying.

Caitlin turned red, furious. If she needed one more reason to hate Robert, she'd just found it.

"Can we leave?" Polly asked. "I want to go home."

Caitlin was relieved to hear those words, but after hearing the story, she wasn't quite ready to go just yet. "Of course, she said, "but can you just give me one minute?"

Polly nodded through her tears, her makeup running, and Caitlin strutted through the room.

She spotted Robert easily—he was the easiest one in the room to find, with that huge white feather protruding off the back of his mask, three feet higher than anyone else. She saw him giggling as he danced with several girls across the floor.

Caitlin spotted a passing server, reached over and grabbed a silver goblet overflowing with champagne, and hurried towards him. She snuck up behind them, and as he was dancing, casually pretended to trip, and dumped the entire goblet of champagne down his back. She made sure she dumped it down his neck, so that it trickled down his bare skin.

Robert shrieked, and pranced about the room, hopping from one foot to the other, as the cold liquid trickled down his bare back.

Caitlin ducked into the crowd and hid herself. Robert wheeled, again and again, looking for the offender, but it was futile. The girls all around him laughed at him.

Caitlin, satisfied, set the goblet down and hurried back towards Polly.

The room was really emptying out now, and a new song started, a slower, more romantic one—probably, Caitlin assumed, the last song of the night. She looked over and saw that Mozart was still playing, sweat pouring off his face, pale, not looking very healthy.

And that was when she felt it.

The fingers on her shoulders. The electric thrill as it passed through her.

She stopped in her tracks. She was afraid to turn around and face him. Afraid that it was really him. And that she would lose him again.

Slowly, she turned.

And there he stood, with the same gold mask. With one hand outstretched, waiting for her hand. He had found her. For the last dance of the night.

Her heart pounding, Caitlin took his hand, as he placed his other on her waist. She held his hand tightly this time, and put her other on his shoulder, determined not to let anyone break them apart.

They waltzed slowly across the room, and with each step, she felt her heart soaring through her chest. It was really him. She was so happy that he was alive. That he had made it. It reaffirmed her belief that everything had a reason. That, no matter what came between them, they would always be destined to be together.

The dance went on, as slowly, the room emptied.

Finally, the dance died down, and they stopped, each holding the other tightly, neither willing to let go.

Finally, he released his grip, raised his hand, and prepared to lift his mask.

Caitlin's heart pounded so hard, she could barely even think.

He pulled his mask back.

And that was when Caitlin fainted.

CHAPTER ELEVEN

Kyle flew quickly in the night, diving right for Venice. That priest had been a tough one—it had taken more severe torture than Kyle had imagined to get the answers out of him, to find out where Caitlin had gone. But in the end, right before he killed him, Kyle prevailed. He smiled at the thought of it.

Kyle dove for the back streets of Venice. It was a fast and hard dive, and he chose an unlit alley, one that he'd always used whenever he'd needed to visit this stinkhole of a town. Just as he remembered, the alley was filthy and pitch-black. It provided the perfect cover for landing in the night.

It was so dark that Kyle couldn't precisely see where he was going, and he came in a bit too fast, and accidentally set down on something. At first he was surprised by the softness of the ground, but when he heard a man grunt, he realized he'd landed on a sleeping bum.

The bum jumped up, and scowled back at Kyle. "What do you think you're doing!?" he screamed.

Kyle, annoyed already, didn't give him a chance to finish. He kicked him hard, and sent him flying across the alley, hard into a wall. The bum collapsed, unconscious. That made Kyle feel just a bit better.

Kyle looked around, and, with satisfaction, noted that no one had seen him land. As he headed down the alleyway, he recoiled at the smell, the stink of this city. It almost made him pine for the 21st century.

Kyle straightened his shirt, and walked out into a square. He found himself smack in the thick of the crowds of Venice. The human fools danced and played and sang all around him. It irritated him beyond belief. He couldn't fathom what they could be so happy about. They were just a bunch of mortals, with no purpose of life, like he had. None of them were driven, set out to achieve things, worked nearly as hard as he.

The more they laughed, the more that he felt they were mocking him. His fury rose. He picked out one of them from the crowd, a particularly happy clown. He crept up behind him and kicked him hard, right behind the knee, and sent him to the ground, his juggling balls scattering everywhere.

The man spun and looked all around to see who did it, but he could not figure it out in the crowd. At least he had stopped laughing. That made Kyle smile, and lifted his spirits just a bit.

Kyle elbowed his way through the crowd, across the square, then down another alleyway. Finally, he reached the waterfront, and made his way along the docks. It was slightly less crowded.

And there it was, just as he remembered it: the Bridge of Sighs. A small foot bridge, with maybe 20 steps on either side, and a fifteen foot bridge, it was just high enough for small boats to pass under. It stood opposite a prison, and from here, one could watch as prisoners were hauled off to jail. The bridge got its name, Kyle remembered, from the "sighs" of the loved ones who would stand and watch their people being taken away. It was one of Kyle's favorite places in Venice.

More importantly, it was exactly where he needed to be. Before he could track Caitlin down, he wanted to first wreak havoc on this dump of a town. Not only because it would give him great joy to do so, but also because it was pivotal to his plan. He needed a distraction. He didn't want to have to encounter her entire coven head on, by himself; he didn't want to risk getting outflanked, and missing the girl again. He needed some back up. And since the Grand Council wasn't going to give him any, he needed to create a plan of his own: the jail. Once he opened their cells, they would tear the town to pieces. That would more than suffice to provide the distraction he needed to keep the humans and the covens' hands full.

Kyle descended the bridge, made his way down the alleyway, through a backdoor, and into the large structure housing the jail.

He strutted down the empty, marble corridor, and headed to a flight of stairs. Down there, he knew, in the bowels of Venice, sat the city jail. There he would find hundreds of human prisoners to let loose, to wreak havoc on the city—and even some prisoners of his own race.

Several policemen stood guard before the staircase, and stiffened as he approached. One of them began to raise his bayonet.

But Kyle didn't give them the chance. He suddenly leapt in the air, kicking one hard in the chest. In a whirlwind of speed, he punched and elbowed the others before they could react, tore the bayonet from another's hand, and stabbed them.

Within moments, all the guards lay before him, dead.

Kyle quickly looked each way, reassured he had not been watched, and hurried down the flight of steps.

This was going to be a beautiful night, indeed.

CHAPTER TWELVE

When Caitlin opened her eyes, she found herself looking up at a ceiling. It was so high, so far away from her, and she noticed it was beautifully painted in a fresco. She was so disoriented, she tried to remember where she was. She felt that she was lying on her back, and felt that her head was in someone's lap. Immediately, she remembered.

She looked up, blinking, to see who it was, her heart racing.

But staring back down at her was not Caleb.

It was Polly.

Caitlin sat up quickly, shaking off the cobwebs, looking all around.

"Finally," Polly said. "I thought you'd be out forever. What happened?"

Caitlin looked all about the room, scanning the masks of the crowd that was quickly petering out. A pang of terror raced through her.

"Where is he?" Caitlin asked.

"Who?" Polly asked.

She scanned the room again. *No. This could not be happening. Not again.*

Caitlin thought back. She tried to remember the moment when he lifted the mask. Looking into his eyes.

It hadn't been Caleb. And that was what had shocked her most of all.

No, Caleb had not appeared, at any time in the night.

The man facing her, the man she had danced with, the man she had felt such a connection with, was Blake.

And now, he was gone.

She was so mad at herself. Why had she had to pass out? Why did things like this always happen to her, at just the wrong moments?

"I saw you faint," Polly said, "and saw a boy catch you, and I came over to help."

"Where is he?" Caitlin asked anxiously.

"Once you were safe in my arms, he disappeared."

Suddenly, another voice came: "Only for a moment."

Caitlin wheeled, and her heart stopped in her chest.

Standing there, just a few feet away, was Blake. He slowly removed his mask, and stared back at her with the same intensity he had before, the same intensity she remembered from the very first time they'd met.

It all came flooding back. Their guard duty together on Pollepel, his cello playing, that night on the beach, their talk—she remembered all of it as if it were yesterday.

She wondered if he remembered, too. The way he looked at her, it made her feel as if he did.

But then again, how could he? That was in the future, and now she was in the past. Unless he had the power to see into the future. It seemed that most vampires had it, some stronger than others, so, she reasoned, it could be possible for him to remember, or, rather, to see into the future.

"Yes," he said, reading her mind with precision. "I do."

Caitlin felt herself blush, once again embarrassed by others reading her mind. At the same time, she felt overwhelmed with emotion, by the fact that he remembered.

He remembers. All of it. He really does.

That alone meant the world to her. Finally, she felt as if she weren't so crazy, weren't so alone. It felt like her first real connection to the 21st century. Finally, she didn't feel like a complete stranger here, like none of it had ever happened.

"Caitlin?" Polly said slowly, bewildered, looking back and forth between the two. "You haven't introduced me to your friend."

Caitlin stood there speechless, not sure what to say.

"Um…" she started, but then stopped. She tried to think of how to explain, but she had no idea where to begin.

So she stood there, speechless, until it got awkward.

"I'm Blake," he said finally, extending a hand to Polly.

Polly took his hand, warily. She looked at Caitlin, who was still staring at Blake as if she had seen a ghost. Not only was Caitlin overwhelmed by this connection to her past—but she also felt overwhelmed by her feeling of connection to him. She'd forgotten how striking he looked.

"You okay?" Polly asked.

Caitlin slowly nodded, still transfixed. That feeling she'd felt when they'd danced, when they'd held hands…she knew it was real. She had felt certain it had been Caleb. The connection had been overpowering. How could it be that it was not Caleb? That it was Blake? And how could it be that Caleb didn't appear the entire night?

Caitlin felt certain that, since Caleb hadn't appeared this night, with her searching so hard for him, with her *willing* him to be there, that he wasn't here. She felt a mix of emotions, as her heart dropped, as the reality began to hit her that Caleb may not have survived the trip. Or maybe he had survived, but had ended up in another time and place.

At the same time, her heart soared at her feeling of connection to Blake. There was so much left unsaid between them. And she had no idea where to begin. On the one hand, she felt disloyal to Caleb to even talk to Blake. But at the same time, it seemed like Caleb was no longer here.

Polly looked back and forth between the two of them, each staring at the other, and seemed to grow uncomfortable.

"Caitlin," she said, "I think you and I should go home now. It's almost five. Most everyone's left already."

Caitlin nodded, but did not say anything, unable to peel her eyes away from Blake's. He was so gorgeous, so perfect, so sculpted, his chiseled jaw standing against his perfect skin. His dark brown eyes shone, looking at her with an energy she had never felt.

"Actually, if you don't mind, I'd like to accompany her for a while," Blake said.

Polly began to protest, but he quickly added, "Don't worry—I'll bring her back safe and sound."

"Caitlin?" Polly asked. "Is that what you want?"

Is that what I want? she thought. It was what she wanted more than anything. In fact, at that moment, she could not imagine herself anywhere else but with him. She felt as if she didn't even have a choice. Like she didn't *want* to have a choice.

"Yes," was all Caitlin, finally, managed to say.

"Do you know where we live?" Polly asked, ever the protective friend.

Blake nodded back. "Of course. Everyone does. Isola di San Michele."

Polly still seemed reluctant to walk away.

Finally, Blake stepped forward, and held out an open palm to Caitlin.

Caitlin hesitated just a beat, and then reached out and placed her palm in his.

CHAPTER THIRTEEN

Caitlin sat in the gondola, as Blake stood on the bow behind her, gently rowing them through the small, narrow canals in the inner city of Venice. It was so late now, the city seemed asleep, completely silent and getting darker by the moment, as more and more street torches extinguished. The only thing left to light the night was the large moon above, and the occasional burning candle in a window sill. Caitlin could only hear the slight lapping of the water against her boat, the sounds of Blake's wooden oar cutting through the water. It was so peaceful, so romantic.

This was a whole different Venice, one Caitlin hadn't yet seen. It was quiet and empty. This was the inner Venice, the narrow canals that cut through the heart of the inner-city, twisting and turning, just like the alleyways did, but on water. Every hundred feet or so, she and Blake would have to duck so as not to hit their heads on a small, stone footbridge. The canals were so narrow, there was barely room for two gondolas to fit side-by-side.

Caitlin looked up as they went, and saw the crumbling interiors of the homes built on the city. They all had doors that opened right onto the water, and most had their own gondolas tied to posts. High above, clothes hung on lines everywhere. This was the quiet interior of Venice, where the locals lived. It felt ancient.

Caitlin wondered what Blake was thinking as they rode together in silence. He was one of the most silent men she had ever met, and it was always hard for her to tell what he was thinking. They had been quiet together for so long. On the one hand, she had a million questions she was burning to ask him; but on the other, strangely enough, she felt very comfortable with him just like this, in the silence. She didn't really feel a need to talk around him in order to be comfortable, and she could tell that he didn't, either. She thought back to their time on Pollepel, of how silent he been then. Nothing had really changed. Centuries could pass, but people were who they were.

Which was all right with her. She was just thrilled to be with him, to be taking this ride. She closed her eyes, breathed in the saltwater air, and tried to freeze the moment. A moonlit, gondola ride in Venice. What more could she ask for?

Finally, though, some questions burned to the forefront of Caitlin's mind, and she just had to ask them. She took a deep breath, hoping that she wouldn't ruin the moment.

"How much do you remember?" Caitlin asked, finally.

The question hung in the air for what seemed like forever, so long that Caitlin began to wonder if he had heard it, if she had even asked it.

Finally, his response came: "Enough."

Caitlin wondered what that meant. That was Blake. He was always so cryptic, never saying more than he had to. "Do you remember Pollepel?" she asked.

Again, a silence. Then, finally: "I wouldn't call it remembering," he said. "It's more like looking into the future. Looking into a life that would have been. I see it, intellectually. But I haven't experienced it."

"Then…" Caitlin paused. "Can you see our time together?"

He paused. "Some of it," he said. "It's more like an impression. I have an impression of you from another time that is very strong. The details, though…are hazy. I think they're meant to be. After all, we need to start fresh each time, don't we?"

"And what is your impression?" she asked.

She couldn't see him, as he stood behind her, rowing, but she thought, in the silence, that she could hear him smile. "Very positive," he said.

Then he added, "They say that there are certain people we are destined to see again and again, in every lifetime, in every place….I feel that with you."

Caitlin knew exactly what he meant. She felt it, too. It wasn't a matter of love. It was something stronger. Destiny. Fate. Inevitability. Being *meant* to be with a person, whether you liked it or not. It was that magical moment when the universe *forced* paths to cross, overrode anyone's option of free will. It was that one moment in life when free will was forced to submit to something even bigger, more important. Destiny. And that, she felt, was even bigger than love. Love, she felt, *true* love, she could only have with one person in one lifetime, and that was something she could choose. But *destiny*—she felt that she could have a destiny with many people, and that she wouldn't have a choice.

She was afraid to ask the next question, her heart pounding.

"Did you know I would be here tonight?" she asked.

There was a long silence. Finally, he said: "Yes. That's why I came."

"Are we destined to be together in this lifetime?" she asked.

"I don't know," he said. "But I do know that I want to be with you."

As they turned a corner, the small canal opened up into the huge grand canal. The lagoon spread out before them, its clear blue waters obscured in a mist that hung over everything, making the moonlit glow surreal.

Caitlin's mind reeled. Her emotions were taking over, and she was having a hard time remembering why she'd come back to this time to begin with. It was getting harder and harder to think of Caleb. She had been so set on finding him. But now, she felt certain, more certain than ever, that he just wasn't here. So then why had she come? Was she meant, instead, to find Blake? To be with him?

Blake pulled the boat up alongside the dock, tied it down, and sat beside her. Dawn was breaking, the sky beginning to light up in a medley of colors.

She turned and faced him, happy to be able to look at him finally.

"Time is such a precious thing," he said. "It feels like it lasts forever, but it doesn't. Life twists and turns so fast. One minute we may be together, and the next minute, separated forever."

She thought about that, and realized he was right.

"It's ironic," she said, "that for such an immortal race as ours, time is the one thing we never seem to have enough of."

He stared at her with a burning intensity, and she stared back, overwhelmed by her own emotion.

"I live in a palace in the countryside," he said. "I want you to come with me."

Caitlin didn't know what to say. She was speechless. Her heart pounded in her chest, and she felt her mouth go dry. She didn't have the strength to say no. She felt as if she were standing outside of herself, watching it all happen, that she was just a helpless passenger in the ride.

Blake suddenly leaned forward, and she knew that he was coming in to kiss her. Her world became dizzy, and she froze. She closed her eyes.

And then, a second later, she felt his soft lips touching hers.

And that was when she heard the noise.

They both suddenly broke the kiss and turned at the same time.

There, walking along the pier, was a young couple, swinging a child between them. The child practically bounded with joy against the breaking sky, and both parents' seemed radiant. They were heading towards a boat, just a few feet away from Caitlin and Blake, and as they got there, the father turned and looked their way.

Caitlin's heart stopped.

The man must have been struck by the sight of Caitlin, too, because his huge grin suddenly dropped, and he let go of the child's hand slowly, as he turned and stared right at her.

The woman standing beside him, a tall redhead, turned and stared at Caitlin, too.

Blake, surprised and not understanding, looked back and forth between the two of them.

Caitlin's world had just turned upside down.

There, standing just a few feet away, was Caleb.

CHAPTER FOURTEEN

Caitlin leaned back in the small boat, looking out at the breaking sky of dawn, and wished the world would end. As they headed further out into the Grand Canal, no land in sight, all she could see was water—and a part of her wished that she could just keep going, never stop, into the horizon, and off the face of the earth. She was so sad, so confused…she just wanted to curl up and die.

She had never felt so alone. The person rowing the boat was not Blake, or Caleb, but a complete stranger, a gondola driver that she had found at the pier, who she'd hired to bring her back to Polly's island. Luckily, Polly had given her money earlier in the night, in case anything happened.

Blake had insisted on at least taking her home, but she had refused. Her feelings for him were too strong, and after seeing Caleb, she couldn't bear to be in a boat with him for one more second. She needed a chance to sort out her feelings, to try to process it all.

The irony was that, if they hadn't run into Caleb at precisely that moment, Caitlin felt sure that she would still be in a gondola with Blake, maybe on the way, right now, back to his palace. They would probably have had a beautiful night, one which she would have never forgotten, no matter how long she lived. If she hadn't had run into Caleb at that moment, she may have even spent the rest of her life with Blake.

But clearly that was not meant to be. It just wasn't destined.

No. At that exact moment, at the exact second that Blake's lips touched hers, at the moment she had finally given up on finding Caleb, destiny had to have Caleb cross her path. He had been out for an early morning boat ride, with his wife, and their son. They had been up early, the eager boy, anxious to get out on the boat, to take a morning ride.

Why had she had to notice him? And why had he had to notice her? And why did it all have to happen at the exact moment when Blake's lips touched hers? Not only did she now feel more confused than ever about Blake, but she now also felt like a traitor to Caleb, like she had done something terrible. Did life have to be so cruel?

When she first spotted Caleb, after overcoming her shock, her guilt at kissing Blake, her first feeling had been joy, overjoyed to see the Caleb was alive, and in this place and time. She had jumped out of Blake's boat without thinking, nearly tipping it over, and had run across the pier, right towards him, and had stopped herself just a foot away.

She had stared up at him, and he had stared back down at her. At first, she could have sworn she saw something like recognition flicker across his face.

But a second later, his face contorted to something like bewilderment. He continued to stare at her, but it wasn't the stare of a lover, or even of a friend. It was the stare of someone who might have met you once, but who couldn't figure out who you were.

"Who's that, Daddy?" the boy, maybe ten, had asked, tugging at Caleb's sleeve.

Caleb had ignored him, staring at Caitlin. Finally, Caleb, still looking at Caitlin, had said, "I don't know, Jade."

Caitlin could tell from his voice, from his demeanor, that he really, truly, didn't know. And that was what had hurt her more than anything, hurt her worse than if she had been killed a million times. Here she was, she had come all the way back in time just for him, had put her life on the line, had lost their child together—and all for what?

On the one hand, it had worked—he was alive and well in another time. For that, she felt a huge sense of relief.

And yet, he no longer knew her. Aiden had warned her of this. He had said that time travel was unpredictable. Blake, who she barely knew, had remembered her. Yet Caleb, who she loved more anything, had not. It was too cruel.

At first she'd hoped that Caleb just needed some time to remember—but as she stood there, staring, recognition never crossed his face, and she felt more and more like a fool.

"I'm sorry, but do I know you?" he'd finally asked.

Sera had walked over, stood beside Caleb, ever protective. She looked happier, softer, than Caitlin had ever seen her. Of course she was. She was a woman in her prime, with her husband, and with their living child. She was not the embittered Sera of the future.

"Caleb?" Caitlin had said slowly, still hoping, even while her heart was breaking. "It's me. Caitlin."

Caleb squinted for a second, then finally, slowly shook his head.

186

"I'm so sorry," he said, "but I'm afraid I don't know you."

Caitlin saw Sera's grip on Caleb's arm, as she impatiently tried to steer Caleb back to the boat. Sera clearly didn't remember her either; yet she still looked very uncomfortable. Possessive, jealous. As if she sensed something. Some things, Caitlin realized, never changed.

"Caleb," Sera had said. "We need to go."

And with those few words, Caitlin, his wife and child piled into the boat, and with a few strong rows, were heading out into the water. As they headed further and further into the canal, Caleb turned around once, and looked at her.

Then he turned back around.

Blake had come up beside Caitlin, standing there. Caitlin, feeling more embarrassed than ever, didn't know what to say.

"Who was that?" Blake asked.

She didn't know how to respond. She was upset that Blake had no memory of him either. Was memory was so selective?

And how could she answer that? Who was he?

Now, as she sat there, being rowed into the breaking sky, heading for Polly's island, she ran it all through her mind, again and again. Her time with Blake; their dance; their gondola ride; their kiss; spotting Caleb…. It all seemed to blend together, and she had a hard time separating it. Why had it all had to happen at once?

She felt at odds, at loose ends. Was her entire journey now purposeless? Now that she'd found him, now that she saw that he was with Sera, that they had a child, what was the point of it all? She felt hopeless, utterly depressed. And she felt so stupid. Of course, she remembered now, that Caleb had once been happily married and had a child back in time. She just hadn't thought it would have been *this* time. Right here, right now. Right at the moment when she was ready to reunite with him.

He was married, and had a child. She had to accept that. That was a sacred thing. He was *taken*. The idea of it hurt her more than anything else, but she just *had* to accept it. It was a bond of marriage, and regardless of what might happen in the future, she could not interfere. She would have to let him go.

If that was the case, then what was the point of her coming back in time? Was it really to find her father, as that priest had said? Was Caleb just the lure to lead her down that path?

Or was her destiny to be with Blake instead? Was that the whole reason she had come back? Was that fate's way of winking at her?

On the one hand, since Caleb was taken, there was nothing wrong, she realized, in being with Blake. But a huge part of her still loved Caleb, still longed for him. The idea of being with Blake still, somehow, despite everything, felt disloyal. *Disloyal to who?* she wondered.

Why had it never entered her mind that things could go so wrong? She had imagined that possibly she could never find Caleb. But she had never imagined that something even worse could happen: that she could find him, and that he could be with someone else. And not even remember her. It was the worst thing she could possibly imagine. She should have foreseen it. But if she had, would she have done anything differently?

Dawn was breaking fully on the horizon now, shades of red and orange and pink flooding the sky, lighting up the lagoon and the water. She had been awake all night long, she realized, and now the world was beginning anew again.

She saw the island on the horizon, and knew she would be there shortly.

But a part of her wished she wouldn't. A part of her wished their boat would just keep going, and fall off the face of the earth.

CHAPTER FIFTEEN

Caitlin ran. The sun was high overhead as she ran through a field of flowers, thousands of roses, impossibly tall, reaching up to her waist. They were all different colors, red and pink and white and yellow, and they brushed against her softly as she ran. Amazingly, they had no thorns, and the feel of the flowers was smooth on her legs, as their smell filled the air.

On the horizon stood her father, taller than ever, closer than she could remember. She could almost make out his facial features, and as she ran, she felt as if she were about to reach him.

But as she looked down, the field of flowers disappeared, and was replaced by a small, golden bridge. Her father, too, was gone, and on the horizon sat a city, with low buildings, all with red tile roofs. The small, golden bridge went up in an arch and came down the other side.

She ran across it, and underneath her, she saw the crystal clear water, glowing blue. She crossed the bridge, about to enter the city, and her father appeared again, at the entrance to the city gates. He stood just on the other side, and as she ran for him, there suddenly appeared two immense doors, freestanding, in the middle of the street, blocking her way.

She knew she could not get around them. They were tall, three times her height, and as she stopped before them, she was amazed to see that they were made of solid gold. They were intricately carved with the most beautiful figures, figures she could not understand. She knew that her father was behind them, on just the other side. She knew that if she could just open the doors, she could reach him, that he was waiting to embrace her.

She searched everywhere, but found no handle. So instead, she reached up, and ran her fingers along the carved, golden figures. She felt the smooth shapes and contours, was amazed at their depth of detail. It was like a piece of artwork.

"Caitlin," came the voice. She knew that it was the voice of her father. It was a deep, soft, relaxing voice. She craved to hear it again.

"I am waiting for you," he said. "Open the door."

"I can't!" she cried frantically.

"Caitlin!"

Caitlin opened her eyes and saw Polly standing over her, shaking her.

Caitlin woke up, disoriented. Had it been her father's voice? Or Polly's?

She sat up and looked all about the room, looking for her father. But it was just another dream. It had been so vivid, like a meeting.

She sat up, rubbing her eyes, and squinted against the harsh sunlight streaking into the room. Daytime. She tried to remember. When had she fallen asleep? Had she been sleeping all day?

Rose came up and licked her face.

"What time is it?" Caitlin asked, groggily.

"It's late in the afternoon," Polly said, "you've been sleeping all day. I didn't want to wake you. I let you sleep as long as I could. But now, most the day's passed, so I figured it's ok. You've slept enough, right? I'm just dying to talk to you. How did everything go last night? What happened? Why didn't you come back with me? Did Blake bring you back? How was your time with him?"

As always, Polly fired question after question, barely giving Caitlin a chance to think. She didn't know which question to answer first.

"I didn't come back with him," she said. "I came back alone. I hired a boat to take me back."

Polly's eyes opened wide in anger.

"What happened?" Her expression darkened. "If he abandoned you there, I'll kill him—"

"No, no," Caitlin said, "it's nothing like that. He *wanted* to bring me back. I asked him not to."

"Why?" Polly's expression changed again. "Oh, I see," she said. "Things didn't go so well? You don't like him? Why, what did he say? What happened!?"

"No, it's nothing like that either," Caitlin said.

She got up, stretching her legs, needing to breathe a bit, to process it all. She wanted to answer Polly, but she barely knew the answers herself.

"I guess I just…needed time," she said. "To think it all over, you know? I actually…I…ran into someone else last night…someone I used to know."

Polly hesitated. "That…Caleb person you were talking about?"

Caitlin looked away, her heart pulling at even the sound of Caleb's name.

"Yes," Caitlin answered, finally.

"So? What happened?"

Caitlin thought. What *did* happen? She still could hardly believe it all. That Caleb did not remember her. It felt like she'd been stabbed in the heart. And seeing him together with Sera, so happy….It was more than she could handle.

"Things…I guess…just didn't turn out as I expected," Caitlin said.

"So? What about Blake? What's wrong with him? You guys seemed to dance so well together."

Caitlin tried to think. Blake was amazing. There was no doubt about that. And her feelings for him—they were very real. Why had it all had to happen at once? She felt so torn, so conflicted. She knew, intellectually, that Caleb was taken, and that it wasn't healthy to dwell on him anymore. But at the same time, to be with Blake, right now, so fast, at this moment…it just felt too soon.

"There's nothing wrong with him," Caitlin said. "I just… I don't know. I guess I just haven't figured it all out yet."

Polly nodded. "I hear you there," she said. "Guys are impossible." She sighed. "Anyway, sorry for all the questions. I was just really curious. I missed you. You have a way of growing on people. Not to mention, it's almost dinner time. And someone very important wants to see you."

Caitlin wracked her brain. Who could that possibly be?

"Aiden," Polly said. "He asked me to summon you."

*

194

Caitlin walked down the outer corridor of the cloister, past column after column, through the low, arched ceilings along the inner courtyard. All throughout the courtyard she could see her fellow coven members training, heard the click-clack of their swords, as they relentlessly sparred with each other. It made her think back to Pollepel, made her realize that nothing really changes over the centuries.

Caitlin continued, heading towards the main church of San Michele, where Polly told her she'd find Aiden.

Aiden. She was excited to see him again, another link to her past, and yet nervous at the same time. Would he remember her? It seemed that some people, like Caleb and Polly, didn't, while others, like Blake, did—or at least somewhat. What about Aiden? He seemed to see more than most, both in the past and the future. She had a feeling that if anyone would remember her, it would be him.

As always, her meeting with Aiden seemed to come at an opportune moment. She herself was brimming with so many questions left unanswered, felt so much at a crossroads. She couldn't stop thinking of her morning's dream, of her father, of those huge golden doors. She wondered what it meant. She felt, more than ever, that there was a mission burning inside of her, and that she needed to be on it. But she didn't know exactly what it was, or where to go. Should she give up on Caleb altogether? Should she be looking for her father? If so, where? And what about Blake?

Was her journey back in time a huge mistake?

Or was it all for a reason?

She felt that if anyone knew the answers, Aiden would.

Caitlin opened the door to the ancient church, and walked inside.

It was completely empty, save for one person, kneeling at the far end of the room, before the altar. Caitlin did not need to go any further to know who it was. Aiden.

She walked down the center of the long aisle, her footsteps echoing.

She stopped a few feet behind him. He knelt there, his back to her, hands raised, apparently in prayer. He was so motionless, so still, she wondered if he was even alive. Before him, at the altar, was a huge cross.

Finally, after what seemed like forever, just before she was about to say his name, he spoke:

"Caitlin," he said.

It was a statement, not a question. As always, he managed to make even the simplest thing mysterious.

"I'm glad to see you again," he added.

As always, it seemed like everything he said could be interpreted many ways. Did that mean that he remembered her?

Caitlin was unsure how to respond.

Finally, he rose to his feet, turned and looked at her. His eyes shone an intense, light blue, and seemed to look right through her. He still had long silver hair and a silver beard to match, and he looked exactly as he had on Pollepel. It was incredible. He seemed like he hadn't aged at all.

"Thank you for taking me back in," Caitlin said. And then, added: "Again."

Aiden broke into a small smile. "This isn't quite Pollepel, is it?"

Caitlin's heart soared. *So. He did remember.* Did that mean he remembered everything?

"What do you think?" he said, in response to her thoughts.

Then: "Follow me."

*

Caitlin and Aiden walked slowly, side-by-side, along the outskirts of the island, right along the water's edge. Caitlin was struck by the tranquility and beauty of the place. The island was covered in a lush, green grass, dotted with

Italian Cypress trees, and, in the distance, lined with small cemeteries. Water was visible from everywhere.

They walked slowly in the silence. Caitlin began to wonder if Aiden would ever talk.

Finally, she could take it no longer. She had so many burning questions she needed to ask.

"How much do you remember?"

"*Remember* is a funny word," he said. "It's more like…seeing what might have been."

Caitlin was alarmed by his choice of words. "*Might* have been?" she asked.

"When you travel backwards, you of course affect your future. Everything is connected. Your future, after all, is only the sum of your past. Whatever you are doing now, your actions last night, this conversation we're having—all of your actions in this time and place—will change the future you would have had. It is all a chain of events. Alter one link in the chain, and the entire chain alters with it. You're changing your future right now, by being here. And you will continue to change it, with every choice that you make."

He turned and looked at her.

"The consequences are infinite. You are not just affecting this time. You are affecting all times to come."

Caitlin's mind reeled with the implications. She felt scared to say anything, to do anything; she felt burdened. Had she made a mistake to come back here? Then again, what choice had she had? To just let Caleb die?

"I'm so confused," she said. "I don't know why I'm here anymore. At first, I thought it was for Caleb. It *was* for Caleb. I wanted to save him. I wanted to be with him. But now…he's with someone else."

Aiden sighed. "Time is a tricky thing, isn't it? You want things to be exactly as they were. But they never are."

"Then tell me," she said. "Why am I here?"

"That is something you will need to find out for yourself."

"But is there a reason? A point to all of this?" she pressed.

"There is *always* a reason. You look through a too-narrow lens. What you still fail to see is that Caleb is just one piece of a very large and complex puzzle. He was the driving force that brought you back, yes. But perhaps he led you back in time for another reason. You assume you brought him back in time. But perhaps all the while, he was leading you."

Caitlin's mind reeled.

"You *do* have a mission, don't you?"

Caitlin stared, and suddenly her dream came back to her.

"I dreamt this morning of my father," she said. "The same dream I always have, but this time, I saw these golden doors. They were so tall, so beautiful. I tried to open them, but I couldn't. I knew that if I could just open them, I would reach him."

"And what did these doors look like?" he asked.

"They were gold, and they had these carvings all over them."

"Scenes from the Bible?" he asked.

As he said it, Caitlin suddenly realized he was right.

"Yes," she said, excited. "How did you know? Do you know these doors? What does it mean?"

"It's meaning is for you to find out," he said. "Those doors you describe, they exist in but one place in the world. Florence."

Florence. Caitlin remembered the priest's words: *you will find your father in Florence.*

"Your father has sent you a message. He wants you to find him there."

Caitlin thought hard. Had she failed in not going there right away? Should she have avoided Venice to begin with?

"Caitlin, you hail from a special lineage. It is not too much to say that the fate of the entire vampire and human races rests in your hands. And yet, you have not fully chosen to embrace your mission. Instead, you chase past lovers. You still follow your heart. As you knew from the start, your mission begins in Florence. It is time for you to embrace your responsibilities. You must lead us to the shield. And find your true father."

"But I don't know how to do that," she pleaded.

"Yes you do," he answered. "You already have the meaning in your dream."

She looked at him. Florence. Those doors. At that moment, she knew that was where she needed to go.

The sky suddenly darkened, and a strong wind picked up, blowing his hair, and his eyes shone with more intensity than ever.

"You cannot escape your destiny."

CHAPTER SIXTEEN

Caitlin stood by herself on the end of the gondola, rowing it across the wide canal of Venice. Polly was worried for her to go by herself, but after much pleading, she had let her borrow her boat. Caitlin felt that she could handle it, and she really needed to be alone. She needed time and space to think. And most importantly, in the place where she was going, she didn't want anyone by her side. It was a place she had to go alone. Rose was the only one she took; she sat at her legs appreciatively, happy, as always to be at her side.

After her meeting with Aiden, Caitlin had realized that he was right. She had to fulfill her mission. She had to at least to try, to get on the road, to follow the clues, to see where it led her.

But at the same time, she realized that she could not embark without closure with Caleb. She needed to know with absolute certainty that he truly didn't remember, that he truly didn't love her, that he was truly happy with Sera. After all she had been through, after all that they had been through together, she just *had* to know. Last night, everything had happened so quickly, perhaps he had just momentarily forgotten. Now, the following day, perhaps things would be different. Perhaps it had all come flooding back to him in the middle of the night.

If she looked into his eyes, now, in the daylight, and he told her again that he didn't remember, or that he no longer loved her, that would be enough. She would be settled, and could go on her way. She would leave Venice behind, and continue on her journey alone. But until then, she still felt in limbo, and unable to move forward.

The sun was setting, and it got colder as she rowed, the current picking up, along with the wind. She rowed more strongly, heading for the island on the horizon, following Aiden's directions. When she'd told Aiden that she refused to move on without seeing Caleb, he had finally, reluctantly, told her where to find him. The small island of Murano, on the outskirts of Venice. But he had also warned her not to go looking for him, that it would bring trouble.

But what else did she possibly have to lose, if she lost him? She had to risk it. She had to follow her heart. She knew it wasn't safe. But then again, love wasn't safe, either.

Caitlin finally rounded a bend, and the island of Murano stretched before her. It was beautiful, unlike anything she had seen. It looked like a miniature version of Venice, except all the buildings were brightly painted in different colors. As the late afternoon sun lit them up, it looked like a living rainbow. It was cozy and cheerful.

As she rowed down the canal, between the small buildings, she felt a sense of peace and comfort. It surprised her that Caleb's coven would choose this place. She would have imagined something more Gothic. As she headed deeper into the island, she looked for the church that Aiden had described: the church of Santa Maria e San Donato. That, supposedly, was were Caleb's coven lived.

She rowed and rowed, her arms getting tired, and after asking a local, was pointed in the right direction. She headed down another small canal, and then the church spread out before her. It all suddenly made sense: here was a massive church in the middle of the small island. It looked ancient, large, semicircular, and foreboding, with columns all around. In some ways, it reminded her of the cloisters in New York. She could understand why Caleb's people would feel comfortable here.

Caitlin tied her boat and got out, Rose by her side, happy to be on dry land.

She walked across the wide, stone plaza, empty in the late afternoon, headed up the steps, and through the front doors of the church.

It was dark in here, quiet. It was another enormous, ancient church, with endlessly high ceilings, and stained-glass windows on every side. There were hundreds of pews, simple and wooden, and all empty. In fact, as far she could see, the entire church was empty. No priest, nothing.

Caitlin walked slowly down the aisle, taking it all in. She finally reached the altar, and looked up, examining it. There was a large statue of an angel on a pedestal, and behind that, on the wall, several huge animal bones. She'd never seen bones that large. They looked prehistoric.

"The bones of the Dragon," came a voice.

Caitlin wheeled.

There, walking towards her in the empty church, was a person she recognized. At first, she could not remember who it was. Then, as he came closer, she realized with a shock: it was Samuel. Caleb's brother.

He looked like he'd always had, with long hair and a beard, serious, straightforward, battle-hardened. He was a somber man, she

205

remembered, but he'd always seemed to be a good person.

He came beside her, and looked up at the wall.

"Legend has it that they are the bones of a Dragon," he said. "Slain by a hero hundreds of years ago. Of course, it is not a legend. They were slain by one of us. Although, of course, we don't take credit for it."

She examined the bones, high up on the wall, and wondered. Then she turned and looked at Samuel. She wondered if he remembered her.

"I'm sorry to trespass like this," she said. "I was looking for someone."

"My brother," he said flatly. It was not a question. She stared into his eyes, and wondered how much he knew.

"Do you remember?" she asked.

He nodded ever so slightly. She wondered if that was a yes.

"Caleb is with his son," Samuel said.

The word *son* came out like a reprimand, and Caitlin wondered if he was giving her a message: back away. Leave Caleb and Sera and their son alone.

"I'd like to see him," she said. "I *need* to see him."

He stared at her, thinking.

"Our coven has lived here for hundreds of years," he said, disregarding her question. "The Murano glass—people always said it seemed inhuman. They wondered how it could be so superior, the best glass in the world. Of course, it is our handiwork. We cannot use mirrors, so glass of this quality is the next best thing.

"We don't thrive in harming others. We thrive in industry, like the human race. We are at peace now.

"But when someone new comes along, someone from another coven, and makes visits unannounced, and seeks to speak to people whom she shouldn't, it can only bring us trouble."

"I don't want to cause any trouble," she said. "I just want to talk to Caleb. *Please*."

"Do you know what makes a vampire vulnerable?" Samuel asked.

She thought.

"It is not humans. It is rarely weapons. It is rarely even other vampires. We can handle our own against most everything." He paused. Then added: "It is love."

Caitlin thought.

"Love is the weak point of a vampire. It can change us. It can lead to our destruction," he said. "You have good intentions," he added.

"But that does not mean it will yield good results."

With that, he turned his back on her and walked back down the aisle.

As she watched him go, she wanted to say a million things, but she was too bewildered by all of his comments. She didn't know how to react.

Then, suddenly, as he was walking away, he stopped by the door. He paused, and then called out: "You will find Caleb by the docks. With his son."

*

As Caitlin walked across the wide, stone plaza, heading towards the pier, the sun began to set, a beautiful orange and red light breaking through the clouds, washing over everything in the surreal light.

As she walked, Rose by her side, she spotted the docks in the distance, and was grateful that the island of Murano, unlike Venice, was practically empty, with very few people in sight.

She couldn't see Caleb, though, and her heart sank. Had Samuel been misleading her? Why had he been so worried about her presence? Had he seen something that she had not? She had an increasingly ominous feeling, given the warnings from them both.

She searched in every direction, but still, no sign of Caleb.

Then, as she looked down, she saw, sitting there, on the edge of the dock, a boy. He looked to be about ten, and as she looked closer, she realized it was his son. Jade.

Jade was sitting there all alone, staring out at the water, his legs dangling over the edge. He was so cute, sitting there, an exact replica of Caleb. It made her heart break, as it made her wonder what her life with Caleb might have been like. It made her think of the child they would have had together, made her again mourn her lost baby. It made her wonder if she'd made the wrong decision to come back in time.

As Caitlin got closer, Jade suddenly wheeled. He was quick and alert, like his father.

She looked down at his burning blue eyes, and wondered if he was human, vampire, or somewhere in between. She vaguely remembered Caleb having told her that, when he first married Sera, she was human. And she knew that vampires could not procreate with other vampires. So she supposed the child was a half-breed. Like she had been.

Indeed, as they stared each other, even from this distance, she could sense a strong kinship with the boy. Her heart warmed, and she almost felt as if he were her own son.

Jade jumped up, his eyes opening wide at the site of Rose. He ran towards her and gave her a big hug, and she was equally delighted at the site of the boy. She reached up her paws, hugging him back, and licking him all over his face.

"What's her name?" he asked, as he stroked her fur. He still had the high-pitched voice of a boy.

"Rose."

"Can I keep her?" he asked.

Despite herself, Caitlin burst into laughter. She had forgotten how unexpected children could be. "Um…I'm not sure. But you can pet her. It's obvious she really likes you."

"Really?" Jade asked, his eyes opening wider. He and Rose played with each other, fake wrestling: he threw her head back and forth, and she pretended to bite his arm, then let go. Caitlin marveled at the site. They looked like two old friends who hadn't seen each other in forever.

"Rose, gentle," Caitlin chided, alarmed at their rough play.

Rose immediately backed off, and ran to Caitlin's side.

"She was just playing," Jade said. Then added: "Who are you, anyway?"

It was hard to concentrate with his eyes on her. He looks so much like Caleb, so intense.

Caitlin could recognize that this was a very powerful boy.

"I feel like I know you from somewhere," he added.

"I'm Caitlin," she said, extending her hand.

Jade reached up and shook it, trying his hardest to look like an adult. Caitlin smiled, and had to keep from laughing.

"I'm Jade," he said.

"What are you doing out here by yourself, Jade?"

"I'm waiting for my dad," he said, then suddenly turned back to the water.

Caitlin looked out, too, but there remained no sight of him.

"He usually comes in around this time. Before it gets dark. Mom said I could come down here and wait."

Jade sat back down where he'd been, on the edge of the dock, his legs dangling off, his back to Caitlin, looking out.

"You can wait with me if you want," he said, tentatively.

Caitlin felt grateful for the offer. She didn't quite know what to say. This was not how she had expected things to go down. If she waited with him, would Caleb be mad to see her sitting there with his son? Would it make the wrong impression? And what if Sera showed up?

Then again, Caitlin didn't know what else to do.

Rose didn't hesitate. She went over and sat beside Jade. Caitlin decided to follow.

The three of them sat on the edge of the pier, looking out at the water, the sun breaking. Jade reached up and stroked Rose's head.

"You're the lady we saw last night, right?" Jade suddenly asked.

"Yes," Caitlin said.

"My mom got mad after we left. She kept asking dad who you were. He said he didn't know. She thought he was lying," Jade said.

Caitlin bit back a smile. Kids were so honest. She was tempted to ask more, but she held off. That wouldn't be fair.

They sat in the silence, looking out, and Caitlin was surprised at how comfortable the silence was between them. It was almost as if he were a part of her family.

"Do you wait for your Dad here every day?" she asked.

Jade shrugged. "Mostly," he said. "He said that when I'm bigger, next year, I can go with him. This island is boring. I want to train. I want to learn how to fight," he said, a determined edge in his voice.

Caitlin looked at him, surprised at the sudden strength in his voice.

"Why would you want to do that?" she asked.

"Because I'm going to be a great warrior one day," he said. It wasn't bravado. He stated it as simply as if he were stating a fact. And Caitlin believed him. She could sense it, coming off of him, off of every pore in his body. This was a proud, young child, a born warrior. He felt like an ancient soul, and a noble being.

"And what does your Dad think of that?"

Jade shrugged. "He wants me to go to school," he said. "I hate school."

Jade's eyes lowered to Caitlin's neckline, then suddenly opened wide.

"Wow!" he exclaimed. "What a necklace. It's beautiful. Can I have it?"

Caitlin reached down and felt her necklace; she had forgotten, as always, that she was wearing it. She was surprised by how transfixed the boy was to it; she felt bad saying no, but she couldn't give it away.

But then again, why couldn't she? And to Jade, of all people? If anyone else had asked her, she would have refused—but there was something about the way he looked at it. Somehow, for some odd reason, it suddenly felt right for her for him to have it. Perhaps, in some small way, it would connect her to Caleb, complete some sort of chain.

She gingerly removed it and handed it to him.

His eyes opened even wider as he took it.

"Really?" he said, clearly surprised that she had agreed. "My Dad would kill me if he knew that I asked you for it. He says I shouldn't ask for things."

Caitlin smiled. "I won't tell."

Jade put it on, and immediately, it looked like he'd always worn it. He was thrilled.

He turned back to the water, and they sat there in the silence, looking out. They watched together as the sky grew darker.

Finally, after what seemed like forever, he turned to her, and fixed his intense eyes right on her.

"Are you going to be my mommy?" he asked.

Caitlin was shocked. She was so caught off guard, she hardly knew how to respond. She was utterly speechless. Why would he ask such a question? Was he seeing something in the future? In the past?

As she opened her mouth to speak, suddenly, a noise came from the water.

"Daddy!" exclaimed the boy, leaping to his feet, nearly jumping out of his skin with excitement.

Caleb suddenly pulled his gondola right up to the side of the dock. He secured the boat and jumped onto pier.

Caitlin quickly jumped to her feet, too, caught off guard by the quickness with which he approached.

Jade hugged Caleb's leg tightly.

"Daddy, did you meet Rose?" he asked.

Caleb looked down, as Rose licked his hand.

Caleb placed a hand on Jade's head, and stared at Caitlin.

He paused. "Jade, can you give us a minute?" he asked, his eyes on Caitlin. "Run home to mommy. I'll be right there."

Jade hurried across the plaza, practically skipping with excitement.

"Come on, Rose!" he yelled.

Rose took off at a sprint after him. Caitlin was shocked. Rose had never left her side before, for anyone. It made her sad, but it also pleased her that Rose had found someone she loved so much.

Caitlin stood there, facing Caleb, who stared back at her with intensity. Her heart pounded, as she wondered what he would say. She had no idea what to say herself.

Did he, finally, remember her?

CHAPTER SEVENTEEN

Kyle hurried down the staircase, deep into the Venice jail, and as he reached the lower levels, he saw that it was exactly as he remembered it. There was a low, arched ceiling, like a wine cellar, and on either side, were dozens of cells, behind thick iron bars. It was loud down here, hundreds of prisoners' hands sticking out through the bars, yelling out to Kyle as he walked down the aisle.

He wasted no time. He tore at the iron bars with his bare hands, and the iron gave way as he bent it back with a groaning noise, just enough for the prisoners to squeeze out. He did this with each cell as he went, opening one after the other, and in moments, the corridor was flooded with rowdy prisoners, thrilled and bewildered. They all looked to Kyle, all seeming to wonder who he was, how they had earned such good luck. They were jubilant, shouting, victorious.

Kyle held up a hand, and they quieted.

"I have freed you all tonight," Kyle began in a loud, commanding voice, "to fulfill a mission for me. The streets of Venice are yours tonight. You will rape and loot and rob and destroy and cause as much trouble as you possibly can. You will not get arrested again, I assure you of that. This is why I have freed you. I have done you a great favor. I expect you to do one for me. Does anyone here object?"

There was a brief, stunned silence.

"What makes you think you can tell us what to do?" suddenly shouted one particularly nasty-looking prisoner, a large bald man with a huge scar across his nose, approaching Kyle threateningly.

Kyle leapt towards him, and in one motion tore the man's head clean off his body. Blood spurted everywhere, as the corpse dropped to the ground.

The crowd of prisoners stared back at him, shocked.

"Does anyone else have any objections?" Kyle asked. It was not a question.

No one else dared defy him.

"Then go!" Kyle yelled.

With a shout, they all scattered like mice, turning and racing up the stairs. Based on their jubilant yells, Kyle could tell they would cause the trouble he wished for.

But Kyle's work was not done. He headed down the corridor, and descended yet a smaller flight of steps.

He arrived in an even lower, subterranean level of the jail, this one darker, more poorly lit, with fewer cells. And dead quiet. A few torches glowed faintly, and he went up close to a cell. He took a torch off the wall, and held it to the metal, and examined it: as he feared, these gates were not made of iron. They were made of silver.

As he held up the torch, suddenly, a face appeared at it—the grotesque face of a vampire of the Lagoon Coven, one of the darkness and nastiest of them all. He had huge fangs which stuck out of his mouth, tiny lips, and eyes that were entirely red. He practically snarled as he breathed. It was a disgusting creature.

All around him, these creatures slowly came to their bars, all grunting at Kyle.

Kyle reached into a pouch on his belt, extracted a powder, and stood back as he threw it onto the silver. He waited, then reached out, grabbed the bars, and tore them off the wall.

A dozen vampires, some of the nastiest creatures Kyle had ever seen, slowly filed out, all pent up, all ready to wreak damage.

"Follow me," Kyle said.

He could feel them all following, close behind. These needed no instructions. Tearing things apart came naturally to them.

Kyle smiled as they ascended, heading for the night.

CHAPTER EIGHTEEN

Caitlin looked into Caleb's eyes. As he stood there, she sensed that some part of him did recognize her, was trying so hard to remember.

"It's strange," he said. "I dreamt of you last night. I hardly know you, yet somehow, I couldn't shake the thought of you."

Caitlin's heart soared with hope.

"Do you remember me at all?" she asked.

"Somehow…I feel like I do," he said. "But…I just can't recall. How do we know each other?"

She paused, debating what to say. Would all of her words, all of her actions, as Aiden warned, now influence the future? What if she said the wrong thing?

She decided to just tell him the truth. This was her moment. It was now or never.

"We know each other in the future," she said, her heart racing.

Would he think she was crazy?

Even as she said it, she wished she hadn't. She worried if, by saying it, she somehow created a rip in time, told him something he wasn't meant to know, affected how things would play out down the road.

He furrowed his brow as he stared back at her.

"We were together once," she added. She couldn't stop herself; it was too late now. "Or, rather, we *will* be together once. I've come back in time to save you. I didn't... I didn't know you'd be with someone else. I didn't know you had a child. Well at least, not at this moment in time...I'm sorry," she said, stuttering, feeling foolish, "I...didn't mean to intrude. I had no idea. I was hoping you'd remember...I guess...I was...hoping things would be different. I realize...I know, this must all sound crazy."

Caitlin, trembling, suddenly felt overwhelmed with emotion. She could no longer control her tears, and she quickly turned to leave.

But as she did, she felt a strong hand on her wrist.

Caleb held her there, stopping her. She could feel the pulse racing through his palm.

Slowly, she turned. Tears poured down her cheeks as she stared into his eyes.

"I'm sorry," he said. "I never meant to hurt you. I do feel something between us. I really do. But I don't know what it is. And…" he said, pausing, "I'm so sorry, but I just can't remember you."

Caitlin nodded slowly, understanding. At that moment, she realized that there was no hope anymore for them. She felt so stupid to have come back, to be standing here, to be intruding in his life this way. She felt terrible. She had been so selfish. She should have just taken last night as closure. Why couldn't she have just moved on?

Now, at least, finally, it was beyond doubt. As much as it hurt, he clearly didn't know her anymore. She had to move on.

"I'm sorry," she said, wiping away a tear, as he loosened his grip.

She turned to go. Then, before she did, she faced him one last time.

"I just want you to know that I love you. And I always will."

And with that, she ran and lifted into the air, her wings sprouting, and carrying her into the sunset.

CHAPTER NINETEEN

As Caleb stood there, watching Caitlin leave, he felt overwhelmed, confused. A mix of emotions swirled within him, as his brain struggled to understand, to remember. He felt certain, somewhere, that a part of him knew this mysterious girl. But he just had no idea how.

As he watched her go, he felt a sadness within himself which he could not explain. He had never experienced anything like it. A part of him wanted to run after her, to call after her to stop. But if she listened, he would have no idea what to say to her. After all, he didn't know her. And he didn't understand his own feelings.

Perhaps he was just going crazy, just letting some irrational emotions, some strange premonitions, take over and get the worst of him. He had to stay strong, he reminded himself, to remain rational. After all, none of it made any sense. He didn't even *know* her.

But as he stood there, watching her, he could not escape the feeling that he was letting someone precious get away. His emotions suddenly got the best of him, and he prepared to take off after her.

He was about to take off at a sprint, to fly into the air, when suddenly, one of his coven members screamed out his name, and came running up to him.

"Did you hear?" his coven member asked, eyes wide in a frenzy. "What's happening in Venice? There's been an outbreak of prisoners. They're tearing apart the city. If we don't do something, all the humans will die."

Caleb furrowed his brow in concern.

"But how is this possible? Who is behind this?"

"We don't know. But there is no time to waste."

The coven member ran off, heading for the water.

As Caleb turned and looked, he saw all his coven members streaming out of the church, out of the surrounding cloisters, heading towards the water. As they did, they broke into flight, their wings sprouting, lifting them high into the air. His entire coven was being summoned.

His brother Samuel came running up. "Did you hear?" he asked, urgently.

Caleb nodded, and as he did, Samuel reached out and handed Caleb his ivory staff, while Samuel donned his golden gauntlet.

"Will you fly into battle by my side?" Samuel asked.

"Always," Caleb said.

Just as they were getting ready to depart, Sera came running out, all geared up for battle, dressed in a thick, skin-tight, black suit, impervious to nearly any weapon, and carrying a short spear. She looked fierce, as she always did before battle.

Caleb was annoyed to see her here.

"We need someone to stay with Jade," Caleb reprimanded. "He should not be left alone."

"I'm not letting you enter battle without me," Sera said. "Jade will be fine. The battle is in Venice, not here. There is nothing to fear. And I've ordered him not to leave the church."

"I don't like it," Caleb said.

"My brother," Samuel interjected, "we have no time to waste."

Caleb offered Sera one last look, but he could see her mind was made up. She was the most stubborn person he'd ever met.

"Fine," he said. "Let's go."

And with that, the three of them turned and sprinted towards the water, and within moments, were flying into the coming night.

CHAPTER TWENTY

Kyle watched with glee as his plan was executed perfectly. All around him, Venice was in shambles. The pathetic humans ran for their lives, as the hundreds of released prisoners terrified them in every direction. Finally, the humans had finished being so happy, had stopped their stupid games, stopped their music, tore off their masks, and ran for their lives.

They didn't get very far. The convicts were on a rampage of looting, raping, and killing, while the released vampires went right for blood. They killed people on the spot, either tearing off their heads, or diving right for their necks and sinking their fangs in deep. They fed and fed, and soon the squares of Venice looked like a battleground. Bodies lay everywhere, storefronts were smashed, tables were turned over...

And it was all just beginning. Kyle had not been this happy in years.

Kyle waited, searching the skies, and as he watched, perched on the waterfront, he finally saw what he was looking for. The sky darkened as scores of vampires flew overhead. It was Caleb's coven, he knew, heading right for Venice. They were so easily led. They rushed to quell the violence, as he knew they would, and in doing so, left their island unprotected. Kyle had sensed Caitlin's presence strongly on that island. Now, finally, he could go and kill her.

As they blanketed the sky, like a flock of bats, and descended to the shores of Venice, Kyle saw his moment of opportunity. He lifted off into the air, the sole vampire flying in the other direction, completely unnoticed, and headed right for Caleb's Island.

His mouth watered at the thought of finding her there, all alone, and capturing her, or killing her slowly.

It was, finally, time for payback.

*

Jade stood at the waterfront and watched the sky. Rose sat loyally by his side, and had not left it once.

Jade knew that he should not have left the church, as he'd promised his mother. He felt bad for breaking his word, but he just *had* to see what was happening, to watch the battle. Battles like this didn't happen often, and he was bursting out of his skin with excitement. He had run to the waterfront the second they'd left, and had watched as his dad had lifted into the sky. He was so proud of him, and of his uncle Samuel, that he nearly felt his heart leap out of his chest.

Yet he also burned with frustration. He would do anything to be among them now, to be flying at their side, carrying his weapons, helping them in battle. He was almost ten, after all. Why didn't they treat him like an adult already? He just wanted one chance. He knew that if he were with them, he would prove himself, too. He couldn't wait for the day.

Jade knew he couldn't go back inside. He was too excited. He would stand there all night if he had to, watching the sky, waiting until each and every one of them returned. There was no place else he could possibly be.

In the meantime, since he was the only one left on the island, he imagined himself as its sole protector, the lone soldier appointed to stand watch, to guard over all of their precious possessions. Yes, he realized, this was a very sacred obligation, and when his father and uncle and mother returned, they would be proud of him. They would all say, *look at Jade: he stood guard for us fearlessly. He's just as great a warrior as us.*

As Jade watched the sky for the slightest fluctuation, there suddenly appeared, in the distance, a lone figure in it, heading his way. Jade's heart leapt. He could tell even from here that this was a vampire, and that it was not of his own coven. Who could it be? he wondered. And why was he heading this way?

Maybe, Jade realized with a pounding heart, that this would be his first test as a soldier. He tensed up, and held his spear high. He reached into his waistband and reassuringly felt his favorite slingshot and small pouch of stones. He had spent many days looking for the smoothest, roundest stones down at the waterside, and they all fit perfectly inside the sling he had created. He'd spent countless afternoons practicing with it, hurling the stones at tree branches, at targets in the water. He had even taken aim at birds recently, and had managed to kill quite a few. No one else took him seriously, but he knew that, with this weapon of his own design, he had become a force to be reckoned with.

As Jade watched, the figure suddenly came very close, diving and landing on the dock before him, just feet away.

Jade's heart pounded and he felt his mouth go dry, as he saw the size of this vampire: he was enormous. He was dressed in all black, in some sort of battle armor, and as his wings retracted, Jade saw how muscular he was. He was even bigger than his Dad. Worse, he looked terrifying: half of his face was completely scarred, as if it had been torn off.

Rose tensed up, too, growling.

Jade again felt along his side, for his slingshot. But his hands trembled, and he was not so sure it would do him any good. This man looked like pure evil.

Jade swallowed.

The man took several step towards him. Jade wanted to step backwards, but he forced himself not to. Instead, he tried his hardest to act like a man, standing his ground, puffing out his chest and raising his chin. He tried to put on his meanest look. He would never allow himself to be a coward. No matter who was approaching him.

"Stop right there and explain yourself!" Jade yelled out, trying to use his fiercest voice. Unfortunately, his voice hadn't yet changed—it was still too high-pitched, and it cracked a bit.

The man laughed out loud, and took two more steps forward.

"I warn you," Jade yelled, "I am the son of Caleb! This is our island! You will do as I say!"

The man stopped, and this time looked genuinely surprised.

"Caleb, you say?" he asked. The man's voice was dark and deep, coming out almost like a growl.

Jade took some comfort in this. It seemed like his father's name had impressed the man.

"That's right," Jade said, emboldened. "And no one lands here without permission. So you had best leave right now!"

Jade again felt his side for the slingshot, but his hands were trembling, and it was hard to feel exactly where it was.

The man smiled back.

"Very interesting," the man said.

The man looked about the island, as if smelling the air, as if trying to sense something. After a while, he seemed disappointed.

"Your father had a visitor. A woman named Caitlin. Where is she?" he asked.

"She left before everyone else did," Jade said. "But she gave me her necklace. It's mine now. She said I could keep it. And if you don't leave now, my Dad will be back any minute," Jade said, throwing out the scariest thing he could think of.

The man scowled, seeming disappointed.

"Where did she go?" he demanded.

"I have no idea," Jade said. "And even if I did, I wouldn't tell you."

The man smiled again, but this time his grin was more evil than before.

"You are a defiant little boy," he said. "Just like your father. Unlike your father, you will pay the price for standing in my way. Your father has caused me grief throughout the centuries. In time, I will kill him myself, with my own two hands. But in the meantime, it will suffice for me to kill you. Let this be a lesson for him."

With that, the man started taking several steps toward Jade.

Jade's eyes opened wide and his heart pounded in his chest. The time had really come: the time for battle. He'd gotten his wish.

But now that it was here, his hands shook so hard, it was hard for him to control them. Hard for him to think clearly, to remember. The slingshot. The stones. He found himself frozen, unable to move.

He wanted to act, but as the man came closer, a part of him was just too scared to actually break into action.

Rose, as if sensing Jade's inability to act, suddenly burst into a snarl, and ran right for the man.

She leapt into the air, and dove right for his throat. It happened so fast, it caught the man off guard. Rose clamped her jaws down hard on this throat, making the man stagger back several feet, shocked. He grabbed at Rose and tried to pull her off, but he was unable. She bit too hard. Blood was everywhere, as she held onto his throat, unwilling to let go.

Finally, the man got hold of her, and threw her off him. He slammed Rose down so hard on the stone that, with a yelp, the wind was knocked out of her. Then, with a scowl, he lifted up his boot, and Jade could see that he was about to crush her head.

Jade broke into action. In one quick motion, he reached into his belt, extracted his sling, inserted a stone and, as he'd done a million times before, he pulled back his arm, aimed right for the man's eye, and hurled it with all he had.

To Jade's shock and amazement, it worked. The stone went flying at lightning speed, and struck the man, only feet away, in one of his eyes, knocking it out of his skull.

The man grabbed his empty socket and screamed and screamed, horrific screams, as blood poured from his head. Jade had saved Rose's life.

But now the man turned on Jade, and looked at him with a snarl from hell. Jade reached down for another stone, but this time he was not quick enough. The man pounced on him with lightning speed, faster than anything Jade had ever seen.

The last thing that Jade saw was his grotesque face, filled with rage and fury, and heading right for him.

CHAPTER TWENTY ONE

Caleb fought with his coven in the streets of Venice, in the midst of heated battle. With Samuel at one side and Sera at the other, he swung wildly with his ivory staff, killing the convicts left and right. The three of them, outnumbered, were charged by a dozen convicts, but these were only humans, and the three of them prevailed.

But Caleb was caught off guard as a dozen vampires suddenly charged their way. He recognized them immediately—they were of the Lagoon Coven, hardened criminals that he thought were rotting beneath the prisons. Their presence immediately alerted him to the fact the someone had released them, had been behind all this mayhem. That this was all a deliberate plot.

But he hadn't much time to contemplate it, because soon, they were in the thick of battle.

Caleb and his men got separated. One vampire leapt for Caleb's face, but Caleb stabbed him in the throat. Another grabbed his shoulder, but Caleb wheeled and head butted him. Still another charged from behind, but Caleb took his staff, and thrust it backwards, its pointed end going right through his throat.

Two more charged at his front, but Caleb pulled the staff back and swung it down, cracking them both hard across the head, and knocking them to the ground.

Caleb caught his breath, and looked over and saw his brother doing well; but Samantha, with her short sword, was jumped from behind. He stepped in and tore the vampire off of her, wrestling it to the ground.

The vampire reached up with his long claws and tried to gouge out Caleb's eyes. But Caleb grabbed them and twisted them around, breaking the vampire's wrist. Caleb then rolled over, grabbed his spear, and punctured the vampire's heart. It died with a horrible shriek.

After minutes of heated battle, finally, they were the victors. The few convicts who survived took off into the streets, while the rest of them were dead in the square. The vampires, too, all lay dead.

Caleb surveyed his coven members, and saw that, while several of them were bruised and beaten, none had died.

Caleb felt a hand on his shoulder, and turned.

Samuel pointed at the sky.

"The smoke," Samuel said. "It's coming from our island."

Caleb and Samantha exchange a worried look at the same moment. With a running start, they leapt into the air, their coven members close behind.

Caleb felt his heart pounding in his chest, more disturbed now than he had ever been during battle. His island was on fire. And his son was all alone.

*

Caleb landed back on his island with all his coven members, and quickly searched for Jade.

"Jade!" screamed Caleb.

He ran to and fro, as Samantha ran to the church, and Samuel ran to the cloisters. They covered all their bases, looking in every direction as they fanned out.

Fires raged everywhere, lighting up the night, and Caleb knew that someone had attacked. He realized now that what had happened on Venice was just an elaborate decoy; that the real target was his island. That they had been tricked.

Caleb scoured the docks, looking everywhere—and finally, he stopped.

And his heart stopped within him.

There, lying before him, was Rose.

Dead.

There was no way, he knew, that Rose would have ever left Jade's side. Unless something had happened to Jade.

Caleb searched again, and there, in the darkness, he saw the outline of a body. The body of a small boy, lying on the stone.

He felt his entire world collapse around him. He felt himself die inside.

He was unable to move, unable to breathe, to think. He felt himself in utter denial, screaming to himself that it could not be Jade.

But even as he began to approach, he knew it could be no one else.

He knelt by the body, and slowly turned it over.

Caleb leaned back and let out a horrible wail, one of an animal that would never recover. It was a wail that filled the night, that stopped the entire coven, and that rose up to the very heavens themselves.

CHAPTER TWENTY TWO

Caitlin flew, the sky streaked with a million colors in the sunset.

After her heartbreaking goodbye with Caleb, she had lifted into the sky and had not stopped flying since. She had cried for hours, but now, finally, the tears subsided, hardened on her face. She was slowly coming to a new, steely resolve. As she had always been in life, she was on her own. She had never been able to rely on the comfort and safety of a father, or brother, or boyfriend.

She had wanted to say goodbye to Polly, and to Aiden and the others. But she couldn't bring herself to. She felt that she had to get as far away from Venice as possible. She couldn't stand the thought of being anywhere near Caleb when he couldn't even remember her. It hurt too much.

She knew she had to get to Florence—she had known that since she'd arrived—and while she hadn't set out for any particular place, she found herself heading in that direction. South. Hundreds of miles away from Venice.

After hours passed, after she had stopped crying, she'd slowly started to ask herself where exactly she was going—and that was when she realized that it was, indeed, Florence. It felt right to her. She had followed her heart, and it had led to heartbreak. Now she needed to fulfill her mission.

She regretted that she had not done it sooner. She had been selfish. Clearly, she was an important person, and she could be of some great service. And the more she thought about it, the more the idea of finding her father stirred in her a new type of resolve. Finding him was something that she had always wanted, and if going to Florence held the answer, she felt no need to hesitate.

The only person in Venice she truly regretted leaving behind without saying goodbye, was Blake. Now that Caleb was clearly taken, she thought more and more of her night with Blake. Their dance. Their gondola ride. There had been something real between them. And she had just thrown it away. He would probably never forgive her, and she'd only wish she'd had a chance to explain it all, to say goodbye properly. But in her current emotional state, she couldn't trust herself to talk to him.

Boys were too hard for her, too confusing. They overwhelmed her emotions, made it hard for her to think clearly. They always seemed to distract her. She had a mission to fulfill, and she'd have to focus. Being on her own would make it much simpler.

Caitlin also felt sad at leaving Rose behind, but before she left, she felt how strong Rose's connection was with Jade. She was in good hands with him. The two of them were clearly meant for each other, and at least it would keep Caitlin connected to Caleb in some small way.

Caitlin cleared a mountain range, and as she lowered, she saw before her, in the distance, a startling site: the massive, sprawling city of Florence.

She dove further, and found herself circling it. It was magnificent, unlike any city she had ever seen. Nestled in a valley, surrounded in the distance by a small mountain range, Florence was flanked by rivers, over which spanned small, beautiful arched bridges. The last light of sunset lingered in the air, and it was just enough to afford Caitlin a magnificent, bird's eye view.

Everywhere were red, shingled rooftops, sloping gently downward, making it look like the city was aglow in red and orange. The buildings were low, most of them not more than a few stories high, and the skyline was punctuated with a plethora of church steeples. Some churches had domes, others, square towers. The grandest church of all towered over everything else, its massive orange, tiled dome seeming to rise up from the center of the city itself.

As she flew close to the city center, she saw huge mansions and palaces, the massive buildings towering over the smaller ones around them. Amidst the buildings, every several blocks, were open squares. She could already see that the city was not nearly as crowded as Venice. Thankfully, there seemed to be plenty of breathing room down below.

Caitlin circled the city a third time, taking it all in. The architecture was beautiful, so clean, so ancient. There were statues in all the squares, and people strolled leisurely, at ease, while others rode on horses. The rivers surrounding the city were aglow in red from the sky, and people casually crossed the many footbridges.

Caitlin had no idea where to begin her search. She had never been to Florence, and the city was so spread out. As she flew, she hoped for some hidden sense to kick in, some intuition, a message, perhaps, from her father. But nothing came.

She decided to approach the city from the outside, to get the experience of entering it for the first time. She also thought it wiser not to land right inside the city, in case she was detected.

She crossed over the river, just as it was getting dark, and landed in the woods on the other side.

Caitlin walked down a dusty dirt road, heading towards the river bank. Her immediate concern was finding shelter, and food. She was hungry. Not for food, but for blood. Being in the forest, and in the thick woods, stirred up her hunger. She could smell deer close by.

Caitlin heard a rustling in the branches, and she turned and saw a family of deer standing there, not more than 30 feet away, staring.

She jumped into action, choosing one, and chasing it down.

As it bounded left, then right, she stayed close on its trail. She remembered her time with Caleb, in Salem, his teaching her how to hunt.

He taught her well: moments later she found herself leaping onto a small deer and sinking her fangs into its neck. It was a direct hit. The deer went down, Caitlin on top of it. It kicked for a few seconds, but then it stopped, as Caitlin sucked the blood from its body.

As she drank, Caitlin slowly felt her life's force returning.

And then she suddenly heard a click behind her—a loud, distinctive click.

She immediately recognized it as the click of a rifle.

She froze, and slowly turned.

There, standing over her, was a hunter, elegantly dressed, holding a rifle, aimed right at her.

"Don't you move," he said to her, threateningly.

Caitlin heard more rustling, and saw that he was accompanied by a group of about 30 humans, all pointing crossbows at her. She was completely surrounded.

She didn't know what to do. She could kill the humans easily enough, but she really didn't want to harm them. She didn't want to have to spend her time here on the run, rushed out of the city before she could find what she needed.

She slowly turned, raising her hands.

"Get up," he said. "On your feet."

She slowly stood, hands held high, debating a course of action. The hunters behind him all seemed itching to fire. The arrows and bullets might not kill her, but they would surely hurt.

"I mean you no harm," she said.

"We know what you are," he grunted. "A vampire. Your kind bring nothing but evil. I killed one of yours just yesterday. Apparently, I didn't kill enough."

The man clicked back the action on his rifle, and raised it higher, right for Caitlin's head.

She realized that he was about to fire.

Suddenly, there was a rustling in the woods, and the entire group spun and looked. A vampire had dropped him from the sky, had landed behind all of them.

Caitlin was shocked to see that it was Blake.

It was the distraction Caitlin needed. Before they could turn back her way, she sprang into action, grabbing the hunter's rifle and tearing it from his hands just as he fired. She had managed to raise it just high enough, so that the bullet missed her head by an inch.

She yanked the gun from him, spun it around, and cracked him across the jaw with the butt of the rifle, sending him down.

Blake had sprung into action, too, knocking three of them down with a single blow.

The other archers turned back to Caitlin and fired, but she was faster than them, and had already leapt into the air. She came down fast and hard, kicking them all in the face. She swung the butt of the rifle wildly, knocking several others over. It would have been easier to kill them, but it was not what she wanted.

Blake was also in a frenzy, punching, kicking, elbowing, knocking them all out.

Of the entire group, only one managed to get off a shot. The arrow pierced Blake's arm, as he let out a scream.

Caitlin spun, identified the hunter, and kicked him so hard, with both her feet on his chest, that he went flying back at super speed, into a tree. To his bad fortune, he went flying right into a sharp, protruding branch, and it punctured his throat. He was pinned to the tree, dead.

All the other humans were knocked out cold, unconscious.

Caitlin turned to Blake, running over to him, feeling responsible for his wound. He stood there, clutching it, the arrow still stuck in his arm.

"Break it off," he said through gritted teeth.

Caitlin hesitated, then snapped the arrow. He screamed as she did.

"Now pull," he said.

She looked at him, unsure, but he nodded, locking his jaw.

In one strong motion, she yanked the arrow as hard as she could. Blake screeched, as it went entirely through his arm. Blood poured everywhere, and Caitlin stopped it with her hands.

Blake reached down, tore a strip of fabric off of his shirt with his teeth, and handed it to Caitlin. She took it, and wrapped it tightly around the wound.

Finally, the bleeding stopped.

Blake bent down, grabbed the tip of the arrow, and held it up to the moonlight.

"As I thought," he said. "Silver-tipped. These were not hunters. They were *vampire* hunters. Looking specifically for types like us."

Caitlin looked at the arrow tip, and saw that he was right. She looked at his wound in concern.

"Will you be okay?" she asked.

He nodded, but not convincingly.

"Let's get out of here," he said.

*

Caitlin stood beside Blake on the stone terrace, leaning against the ornate marble railing. High up on a hill, she looked out over the forest, over the river, at the city of Florence. Her mind was still reeling, still trying to process how she got here, how it all happened.

She had never expected to be surrounded so quickly by a group of humans, especially armed with weapons capable of hurting vampires. She hadn't known of vampire hunters, and it was stupid of her to let down her guard so much. She had been too focused on Florence, too excited to be here—and too hungry, too focused on feeding. It had been a stupid mistake.

Thank goodness for Blake. Seeing him there had been such a shock. She had thought that he'd forgotten about her, and that if he thought of her at all, it would only be with anger. After all, she had left him so abruptly, when he had been so kind to her.

After their encounter, he'd led her through the forest, up this hill, to this incredible mansion. It was, he explained, a palazzo. Sitting proudly high up on a hill, it had a wide, marble staircase, with thick, ornate railings winding their way up to this huge stone terrace. It all led to a magnificent, marble house, with huge oak doors, and glorious arched windows in every direction. Blake had led her inside, and had explained that this was one of his many houses. It was magnificent, fit for a king. It sure beat spending the night in the forest.

After collecting herself and helping tend his wound, Caitlin had wandered out onto the terrace, to get some fresh air, to take it all in. He had wandered out after her, and now stood at her side.

She and Blake hadn't said much, both still reeling from the shock of battle. He looked like he was in pain from the arrow, and Caitlin felt terribly about it. She was deeply touched that he had come for her, that he had saved her. Who knows what would have happened if he hadn't arrived.

They stood there in the warm evening air, each looking out, each lost in their own thoughts.

The silence grew thick, and Caitlin began to feel nervous. She felt her heart start to be faster. She had no idea what to say. She wanted to thank him. But she didn't know how to begin.

"Did you come down here just for me?" she asked softly, in the summer darkness.

He waited several moments, then nodded.

"Why?" she asked.

"I couldn't forget you," he said.

He turned and faced her.

"Our dance. Our boat ride. I thought what we had was real."

He looked at her.

"Was it?"

She looked back at him, at the blazing intensity in his eyes, and could see how deeply he felt things.

"Yes," she answered.

His face seemed to relax.

"Then why did you leave me?" he asked.

Caitlin sighed, trying to think what to say.

Finally, she simply said, "I'm sorry."

"Do you always run when you're interested in someone?" he asked, with a small smile.

She smiled back. "Now that I think about it, I guess I do."

"That's a bad habit," he said, his smile widening.

He turned and looked at the city, and she studied him as he did. He was still very mysterious to her. He was a man of few words, and he was so soft-spoken. She could feel the intensity that burned off of him, and it scared her. He felt like a man who lived life on the edge. He seemed like a hopeless romantic, like someone who was always embroiled in a passionate affair.

"That man you spoke to the other night," Blake continued, "the one with the child. How do you know him?"

Caitlin was at a loss. She had no idea how to explain it. "It's complicated," she finally said.

"Do you have feelings for him?" he asked.

Caitlin paused.

"Yes," she said, truthfully.

She saw Blake's face fall in disappointment.

"But," she added, "that was in the past."

He looked at her, confused.

"What I meant to say was…we're no longer together."

As she spoke the words aloud, it pained her to hear them—but even as she said it, she knew that it was true.

Blake looked at her with a new hope.

"I followed you to Florence hoping that you would say that," he said. "From the moment I met you, I couldn't stop thinking about you. Last night, I visited your island, and Aiden told me you'd left for Florence. I don't know why you're here exactly, but I can sense that you're searching for something. I want to help you. I want to be with you."

He turned and faced her, and took a step closer.

She looked up into his eyes, at his smooth, flawless skin, and felt completely overwhelmed by his presence. She was unable to resist. He looked down at her, reached up, and slowly stroked her face with the back of his hand. She closed her eyes. She remembered that night on Pollepel, that same feeling she'd had. Now it came back, but stronger.

And as he leaned in, and his lips touched hers, she felt her heart swell again. She found herself kissing him back, meeting his lips with equal force.

She found herself melting, and knew that something inside of her was slowly coming back to life.

CHAPTER TWENTY THREE

Caitlin woke to the morning light breaking through the large, arched windows. She reached over to the bedside table, put two drops in each of her eyes, closed them, and waited for the sting to go away.

She opened her eyes and looked around. She saw that she was lying in a huge, king-size bed, in a massive bedroom, with soaring ceilings, moldings over all the walls, and a marble floor draped in a huge, sheepskin rug. She lay on the finest of silk sheets, covered by fine linens and blankets, her head resting in an impossibly soft pillow. She'd never been in such a luxurious place in her life.

And as she looked over, she saw that she was not the only one in it.

Blake lay beside her. And they were both undressed.

She tried to remember. After that kiss, they had gone inside, had spent the night together. It had been a magical night, and thoughts of Blake filled her mind. A part of her, of course, still thought of Caleb.

But that part was slowly fading, becoming smaller and smaller. Lying next to Blake, feeling his energy, she felt she was exactly where she was supposed to be right now.

Caitlin lay there, studying his face, still sleeping, so peaceful. She wondered how far back they went, exactly how many lifetimes they'd known each other.

She finally crawled out of bed, her bare feet feeling good on the cool marble, and walked across the room, to the enormous window. She looked up: the window was at least fifteen feet high, with lace curtains that blew in the breeze.

She leaned out and watched the dawn break over Florence. The river lit up, glowing in the soft light. Birds chirped in the trees all around her.

A strong breeze came in, cooling her down on the warm summer morning, and blowing the drapes back. They billowed in the wind all around her, as she felt the wind caressing her face.

Caitlin looked into the distance, out at Florence, and for the first time in a long time, she looked forward to the day ahead. She couldn't wait to explore the city, to continue the search for her father, for the Shield, especially with Blake by her side.

Finally, she was not alone.

*

Caitlin and Blake held hands as they exited his palace and made their way down the endless marble staircase. She felt like a new woman. She had bathed in the enormous bathtub, and had changed into a new outfit that Blake had given to her. He had actually laid out several outfits for her. She had chosen a simple, black one, not too tight, one which was elegant and yet which seemed to fit in with the times. It had long, black pants, and a light, long-sleeved shirt, all black and all made of a silky material. The outfit was completed by a pair of open-toed sandals. She ached to see what she looked like in a mirror.

She wondered briefly why Blake had all those clothes, but she didn't want to ask, to ruin the moment. After all, she figured, he had been alive for thousands of years, and it was only natural for him to have had past relationships. It didn't bother her, and she was grateful for the clothes.

As they headed down the road, towards the river, it widened, and became busier, the occasional person and horse accompanying them. They blended into the crowd and, held hands. She looked up, and was glad to see that his wound had already healed.

They walked across the small bridge, crossing the river Arno for Florence.

"The Ponte Vecchio," Blake said.

Caitlin looked over at him. He looked happy and content, in his element.

"It is known as 'the gold bridge.' See the merchants? All the little tables? This is where they sell gold. The finest gold in all of Europe. It is not only the entry bridge to Florence, but it also happens to be *the* place to come for jewelry."

As they strolled across the bridge, offering an incredible view of the water and the city, Caitlin looked closely: small tables lined the bridge, around which stood merchants and customers, all examining various piece of jewelry.

He took her hand, and led her to a small booth.

She looked down, and was amazed to see it filled with gold bracelets, necklaces, rings, pendants…. They all shone in the light.

Caitlin fingered a bracelet.

"Try it on," he said, smiling.

She shook her head and put it back. "I was just looking. I don't have any money."

He picked it up.

"*Please*," he pleaded. "Money is no issue for our kind. I have money enough to last one thousand lifetimes, and one thousand more."

Caitlin hesitated.

Blake reached over and placed it on her wrist. It was thin and elegant, the gold a brilliant yellow, and it was lined with small pieces of sea glass. It made Caitlin remember their time on Pollepel, when he had given her that piece of sea glass. Did he remember?

But it wouldn't fit on her wrist.

He tried to open the clasp, but it wouldn't budge.

"You need the key," said the merchant.

She looked up, and saw that he was holding a small key. Blake took it and inserted it into the clasp, and it opened. She was amazed.

"It is designed to be opened only with the key," said the merchant. "Only someone close to your heart holds the key. Only they can open it."

Blake slipped it onto her wrist, then closed the clasp, and locked it. She tried to take it off, but it wouldn't budge.

She looked it over, and held it up to the light. It was beautiful, the sea glass reflecting all different colors. She felt like she was wearing a part of Blake.

"Are you sure?" she asked.

Before she could finish asking the question, Blake had already paid the smiling merchant.

He took her hand, and they continued down the bridge.

*

Caitlin was in awe as they entered the city of Florence. It was one of the most beautiful places she had ever been. The streets were much wider here than in Venice, and not nearly as crowded. They were lined with beautiful façades of buildings, townhouses, storefronts…. People, elegantly dressed, tipped their hats as they walked, and the occasional horse walked leisurely down the street. There were sculptures and fountains everywhere. The streets were lined with cobblestone, and every few blocks they opened into an inviting square. This was a truly a city of light.

"So," Blake asked, after walking in silence, "where to?"

"I need to find my father," Caitlin said. "And an ancient shield. One that he will lead me to."

"Your father was of our kind?"

Caitlin nodded. "I'm told that he came from a special coven. I've never met him."

Blake nodded back. "That's quite common among vampires. Often, the parents abandon the children. It's safer that way. That way, if the parent gets caught or killed, the child is safe. Plus, there isn't as much of a need to be together: the vampire connection is so much stronger between parent and child. Vampires don't need to physically be with their children to be close to them. We can communicate through thoughts, thousands of miles away. And through dreams."

That jarred something, made Caitlin think. Her dream. Those golden doors.

"Actually, that's what led me here," she said. "I dreamt of my father. And these beautiful, golden doors. It was like…I can't explain it, but it was like…like he was pointing me towards Florence. I kept feeling that the answer was behind these doors. They were so unusual, so tall, and beautiful, and they had these carvings all over them."

Blake stopped and looked at her. "You are speaking of the Baptistry doors," he said, with all seriousness. "It can be none other than these."

Caitlin's eyes opened wide.
"Do they really exist?"

"Yes, of course," he said. "They're one of the more famous sites in Florence."

Caitlin's heart leapt with excitement. Finally, something tangible. A real, solid clue.

Blake took her hand. "Follow me."

*

As Caitlin and Blake walked down Via Dei Calzaiuoli, it opened up into a huge square, Piazza del Duomo, and Caitlin was taken aback by the site. Across from them stood one of the largest, most ornate churches she had ever seen. It was built in a light stone, every inch covered with carvings, statues, designs, and interlaced with color—orange and green edgings. It was so ornate, so busy.

Its rear cathedral, rose in an enormous, orange dome—the one she had seen when first flying over the city, the same dome that dominated the city skyline. It was very beautiful, and clearly the most important building in the city.

"Wow," she whispered.

"The Duomo," he said. "The main church of Florence for hundreds of years. Quite overwhelming, isn't it?"

It was. But she didn't see any gold doors.

"But the doors…" she said, "…those aren't them."

"No," he said. "Those doors you speak of are *opposite* the Duomo. In the Baptistry."

He turned her shoulders and pointed. "Look," he said.

Suddenly, Caitlin saw it. There, directly across from the Duomo, sat an octagonal shaped building, which looked small compared to the Duomo, yet which was still quite large, about one hundred feet in diameter, and rising about a hundred feet high. It was as ornately carved as the Duomo itself, in a matching stone and matching colors. But what made it special, what made it eye-stopping, was its magnificent, tall doors. All bright, shining gold. All elaborately carved, with images all over them.

Exactly as Caitlin had seen in her dream.

Her heart pounded. It was so surreal to see something in real life that she had only dreamt of. Now, more than ever, she felt that it was a message, that she was close, once again, to finding her father.

In a daze, she walked up to the doors, and slowly held out her hand and touched them.

It was just as she remembered. She couldn't believe how smooth the metal felt. She marveled at all their shapes, at the intricate detail.

Blake came up beside her. "This is the oldest building in Florence," he said. "Built in 1100. It took them 21 years just to build those doors. All by hand. They look like gold. But they are actually bronze."

She looked up, and marveled at how high the doors went. She looked closely at the depictions, at the small shapes of people and animals and angels.

"These figures," Caitlin asked. "What are they?"

"Scenes from the Bible," Blake answered. "The Old Testament, mainly. You see: there is Moses, receiving the tablets of God."

Caitlin looked closely. She saw angels, demons, people standing with wings….It made her think of her kind.

"Yes," Blake said, reading the thoughts. "Our kind are included. Do you really think a human could have carved these? These doors were carved by one of us."

Caitlin surveyed them in wonder.

"My dream…it told me that my father would be behind these doors."

Blake opened one of them.

Caitlin pulled back the other, slowly. It was heavy, made of solid iron.

"Let's find out," he said.

*

It was dim inside the Baptistry, light coming in only through the stained-glass windows. Caitlin looked up at the high ceilings, and in here, she could really see the effect of the octagon-shaped building. The panels of the ceiling, all brightly colored in frescoes against a gold background, came to a point, with a small circle in its center. Their footsteps echoed on the beautiful marble floor as they walked, and as she looked around, she saw other people milling about. Sightseers.

Despite its great beauty, Caitlin could find no hidden messages, nothing of any great significance. It was basically just an empty structure, with a small altar at one end of it. And her father, of course, was nowhere in sight.

She looked around, again and again, looking for any clue, any message. Frustrated, she finally gave up.

"I don't see anything," she said.

"Neither do I," he said.

She thought again and again.

"What exactly happened in your dream?" he asked.

She thought of her dream again, tried to remember every last detail, wondering if she'd left anything out.

Suddenly, it struck her.

"What if the answer doesn't lie *behind* the doors?" she asked, excitedly. "What if the answer is the door itself?"

He looked at her, puzzled.

She took his hand and led him out of the building.

They stood back outside, before the doors, and she stared intensely at all the carved figures. She circled the structure slowly, walking all the way around, inspecting each and every door. Each had different carvings. She could feel the electricity running through her veins. A message was embedded in one of these carvings, she knew it.

She ran her fingers along them as she walked, trying to sense which one it could be. She closed her eyes, and circled the structure again and again.

Finally, she stopped, feeling something. She opened her eyes and stared.

There it was. Before her was a carved figure of a structure, an old church, with a distinctive shape, tall, capped by three triangles, before which knelt a winged figure. To humans, it might look like an angel, but she knew it was one of her own. This was it. She felt certain of it.

"This place," she asked Blake urgently, breathless. "What is it?"

He came close, examined it. "That is the church of Santa Croce. It's not far from here."

She felt it, more strongly than she ever had. Her father was here. And that was where she had to go.

She turned and took his hand. "Let's go."

*

Caitlin's heart swirled with a range of emotions as she continued down the streets of Florence with Blake. She felt she was coming close, once again, to finding her father, and her heart beat faster at the thought of it. It also brought up a whole series of questions. Had he been living in Florence all this time? What had he been waiting for? What was he like? After he gave her the Shield, would that be it? Would it be over? Or would they be able to spend time together, as father and daughter?

Most of all, would he love her? Be proud of for? In her dreams, she felt that he was. But this was real life. Would it be the same?

She also felt nervous about Blake. Just being with him, holding his hand, walking down the streets of Florence, she felt so at peace, at ease.

She had been so heartbroken over Caleb, and now it felt so good to have a man by her side.

But it had all happened so fast, and it was so hard to think clearly around him, and she still couldn't quite sort it all out in her mind. Did she love Blake for who he was? Or did she only love him now because of what had just happened with Caleb? She wanted to get clear, to know that she truly loved him for *him*; but given her current state of emotions, it was so hard to tell.

Whatever it was that they had together, she didn't want it to end. At least for the moment, it felt right. She wanted him by her side.

But as they continued walking through the majestic streets of Florence, each block more romantic than the next, she couldn't help but worry that this would all soon come to an end. She wanted to freeze this moment, to make it last—but she knew that, like everything else in her life, it could not. She feared for what could happen next. What if her father really was there? What about Blake? Would he stay? And did he plan on sticking around? Or flying back to Venice? She was afraid to ask him. She didn't want to know the answer.

But in the back of her mind, she suspected that she already knew: nothing could last forever. They were on a beautiful, amazing journey together, but eventually, she feared, she would find what she was looking for, and he would have to go back home. When or how they parted ways, she didn't want to contemplate right now. She just wanted it to last. She wanted so badly for everything to last.

And this tainted her enjoyment of the moment. She wished she could push all of her worries out of her mind, and just enjoy the moment, just enjoy the beautiful weather, the breeze, walking down the idyllic streets of Florence. And she did enjoy it. But not as fully as she would have liked. She couldn't help feeling as if she were just in the eye of the storm.

She also felt worried because, for the first time in a long while, she felt at home. As much as she had disliked Venice, she loved Florence. It felt so comfortable, with its red tiled roofs everywhere, its abundance of art, its amazing architecture, fountains, rivers, bridges....For the first time since she'd come back in time, she felt really at peace, at home. She wanted to live here. She wanted to settle down, in one place, one neighborhood, one time. She wanted one family, one husband, to call home. Would this all be taken away?

As they turned down another side street, it opened up into a huge square, with a sign that read "Santa Croce." It was one of the bigger squares in Florence, sprawling for hundreds of feet, and lined with stores and cafés. It was dominated by a huge church, nearly as big as the Duomo, with similar coloring. It rose up in a distinctive shape. She recognized it immediately from the image on the doors. This was it.

"The church of Santa Croce," Blake said, looking at it. "A very special place. It is the burial ground for many luminaries, including Michelangelo and Galileo. It is also home to a cloister."

Caitlin felt more sure than she ever had. Whatever secrets she was searching for, she would find behind those doors.

They circled it, taking note of all the entrances. As they walked behind it, Caitlin saw that the structure stretched backwards for hundreds of feet, and saw, attached to it, the cloister.

"Our kind once lived here, for thousands of years," Blake said. "It is a very special place."

"And now?" Caitlin asked, her heart beating. She wondered if her father was living there now.

"I don't think so," Blake answered. "I believe it was abandoned centuries ago."

Caitlin found a large, arched door leading to the cloister. She reached up, grabbed the metal ring and knocked. The sound reverberated throughout the courtyard.

She tried to open the door, but it didn't give.

She looked over at Blake and he nodded back. She looked both ways, then leaned back and kicked it in. The door went flying open. They hurried inside, and she closed it behind them.

It was dark in here, lit only by the sunlight streaming in through a small window. It took a moment for Caitlin's eyes to adjust. Once they did, she saw how beautiful it was. Like most cloisters she had been in, it was made of simple stone, with low arched ceilings, a courtyard, and open-air arched windows all along its side. A narrow corridor ran along the courtyard.

As they walked it, Caitlin looked at the interior, rectangular courtyard, lined with neatly trimmed grass. On all four sides of it were arched walls, so typical of cloisters. It was tranquil, very serene, and very empty. She felt like they had the place to themselves.

"It's empty," Caitlin said with disappointment. "I don't sense my father's presence. I don't sense anyone."

They walked down another corridor. As they walked, Caitlin noticed how much it felt like the cloisters in New York, and the cloisters on Isola di San Michele. They were all so medieval, so spare, so empty.

"I'm sorry," Blake said, finally. "He's not here."

Caitlin sighed as she surveyed the walls, looking for any sign. Nothing.

"I've heard rumors of this place," Blake said. "A very powerful coven lived here once. Centuries ago. Maybe your father was a member."

"Maybe," Caitlin said, looking around for any possible clue.

Finally, she realized there was nothing more to find here.

"Let's see the church," she said.

*

As Caitlin entered the main church of Santa Croce, she felt a wave of energy. She closed her eyes and felt a tingling in her hands and feet, felt an almost palpable electricity in the air. She was positive that whatever it was she was meant to find was in this room.

"What's wrong?" Blake asked.

She stood there, frozen, and slowly opened her eyes.

"It's here," she said. "Whatever he wants me to find. It's in this room."

Blake surveyed the room with a new sense of wonder. So did Caitlin.

The church of Santa Croce was a remarkable feat of architecture. It was the largest that Caitlin had ever entered. The main room was hundreds of feet long, with a ceiling hundreds of feet high. The enormous room was lined with gigantic columns, and all along its walls were painted beautiful frescoes. The floor was marble, and enormous stained-glass windows allowed in a beautiful, fractured light.

As she walked along the edge of the room, she look closely at the walls, in amazement. Lodged into it, in small alcoves, were sarcophagi. Elaborately carved, these sarcophagi look much like the ones she had seen in the cloisters in New York. They looked like a perfect resting place for a coven of vampires, and she could imagine, back in time, their living here. Indeed, as she looked at them now, she almost felt as if vampires would rise from each one of them.

But as she walked, what really struck her was the floor. There, in the distance, was a series of shapes, protruding from the floor. As she got close, she could see that it was a cluster of tombs, embedded in the floor, marble shapes of human beings, supine, rising up from the floor itself. It was as if the floor were a living graveyard, as if these bodies were getting ready to rise. She thought of the sarcophagi in the

271

cloisters in New York, and she felt certain that this was a sacred place for vampires.

She sensed an energy coming off of one of them, and she leaned in close, and read the inscription. Her heart stopped.

"What is it?" Blake asked, coming close.

"That sarcophagus," Caitlin said. "The name on it. Elizabeth Payne."

Blake looked at it, then looked back and Caitlin.

"Who's that?" he asked.

"My mother," she said, staring. "They say vampires can be buried in many places. This is the second tomb of hers that I've seen." She looked closely around the room. "I don't know what it means, but I know that I'm in the right place."

Caitlin scrutinized everything in the room with a new perception. She scanned the frescoes, the statues, the altar, the sarcophagi, looking for something, she didn't know what. But she felt certain she'd know it when she saw it.

And then suddenly, she did.

She couldn't believe it. There, in the center of the room, beside a large marble column, was a limestone, circular staircase, twisting and turning, winding its way up, about fifteen feet, to a large, stone pulpit. It looked exactly like the pulpit in the King's Chapel in Boston. The pulpit where she'd found the Sword. But this one was larger, and entirely carved of stone.

As Caitlin stared at it, she knew that the answer she sought was inside it.

She found herself pulled towards it, like a magnet, and found herself climbing, ascending its stairs. As Blake watched, she twisted her way higher and higher, and finally reached the top.

At the top was a small, circular landing, and from up here, she had a commanding view of the church. She wondered how many priests had stood up here during the centuries.

She examined its small, stone walls, its ledges, looking for a clue, anything. Remembering the pulpit in Boston, she reached out and felt the walls carefully, checking for a secret compartment.

Suddenly, her fingers ran across something that didn't feel quite right. It was the tiniest crack, between the marble. She slid a finger in, running it alongside it, looking for a secret latch.

She found it. It was the tiniest lever. She pushed it as hard as she could.

As she did, she heard the hissing of sealed air, released for the first time in centuries. She pulled at the stone, and there, indeed, was a secret compartment.

She looked inside, and her eyes opened wide in amazement. She was utterly shocked by what she saw.

But before she could react, Caitlin felt herself constricted.

Disoriented, she looked up, trying to understand what was happening, and as she did, she saw a silver netting, seemingly dropping from the sky, encasing her, wrapping around her. She saw a dozen vampires, tightening it around her, and felt herself falling to the ground.

She looked up, and the last thing she saw was Kyle, standing over her, half his face disfigured and missing an eye. He looked down at her with an evil grin. He lifted his foot, aiming for her face, and she saw it coming down, getting closer, and closer.

And then her world was blackness.

CHAPTER TWENTY FOUR

Caleb stood in the rear of the funeral gondola, standing straight, chin proudly forward, as he rode with as much dignity as he could muster. Lying in the boat before him, wrapped in a black shroud, was the body of his boy. It was a boat just for the two of them, the customary funerary gondola, all-black, and longer than usual.

Sera would not join him. She had been inconsolable, and she had blamed Caleb. Although he was the one who'd asked her to stay with Jade, she was being irrational, and faulted *him*. She'd refused to attend the funeral, and refused to even be in his presence. She'd insisted on a divorce.

Caleb was reeling. It was so much at once, but the greater pain, to be sure, was Jade. He and Sera had been at odds lately, anyway, and he knew the day was fast approaching of their divorce. But Jade—that was a different matter altogether.

Caleb did his best to hold back his tears, but it was a futile effort. He had loved this boy more than he could ever possibly express, had seen all his hopes and wishes and dreams in him. It was not possible for full-blood vampires to procreate, and this boy had been the product of his union with Sera before he'd turned her. It was an illegal union, which was later sanctioned, and thus Caleb was one of the few vampires who actually had a child. But a child like this would never come along again, he knew. As he rode, as he looked down at the body, he knew that all his hopes and dreams would be buried with it.

More than that, he truly loved the boy. He had a warrior's spirit, a heart bigger than any adult he'd ever met. Caleb had been proud not only to be his father, but also to know him as a friend, as a compatriot on this Earth. It devastated Caleb to know that he would no longer be with him. He would miss waking up to his being there, his companionship, their conversation. It was like a part of Caleb had been chopped off.

Next to Jade, also wrapped in a shroud, was Rose. Even in the short time they'd spent together, the two of them had a stronger connection than he'd ever seen. He knew that being buried together would be what the boy wanted.

As Caleb rowed, his entire coven rowed with him, hundreds of funerary gondolas, all-black, right behind him. Samuel rowed closest. They all headed solemnly through the grand Canal, heading towards the Isle of the Dead.

As they reached the island, the water gates opened wide to greet them. It was a rare thing for two vampire covens to come together on any issue, but in this, they were all unified.

Dozens of additional funeral gondolas waited to greet them, Aiden's coven anxious to accompany them, to pay their respects. Aiden stood in the lead boat. As Caleb rowed through the middle, they accompanied him and his people.

When they finally reached the plot of land set aside for Jade, they all, as one force, accompanied the boy and Rose to their final resting place. Church bells tolled in the background, and wails of grief rose up.

Aiden presided over the ritualistic vampire burial, as Caleb personally shoveled the dirt.

"…to resurrect another day," Aiden finished chanting, "in God's ultimate grace."

Caleb stood there, tears in his eyes, feeling surreal, out of touch with his body.

Person after person walked up to him, to try to offer condolences. But there were none to be had.

As Caleb stood there, his grief slowly morphed to anger, to a slow, quiet rage. His boy had been killed. He had not died accidentally, but had been deliberately killed, in cold blood. It was the work of an evil vampire coven, one that had set out to destroy Caleb, and had found his boy instead. Caleb wanted revenge. He *needed* revenge.

And he was not alone. His entire coven demanded vengeance, too, as did Aiden's coven. This was an attack on all of them, and was completely unacceptable. The covens were united.

Caleb finally cleared his throat, and spoke up in a loud voice.

"My fellow members," he began. "What happened today was an attack not just on me, not just on my son, but on all of us. The malevolent coven coordinated this attack, this breach of our shores, and we must answer with equal force. I will fly today to exact revenge on this horrible, unjustly murder. To exact revenge for all of us. If need be, I will fly alone. But I welcome you to join me, to avenge the cruel and merciless death of my innocent boy.

"Are any of you with me?"

A huge roar of approval rose up, and Caleb's heart swelled at the support.

"Then fly with me now!" he yelled.

With that, Caleb took three steps and flew off into the air, by himself.

It took but a moment for him to hear the fluttering behind him of thousands of wings.

It was an entire army, mobilized for war.

CHAPTER TWENTY FIVE

As Caitlin tried to open her eyes, she had a splitting headache. She slowly raised her head and looked about, trying to get her bearings. She blinked several times, and realized that she lay curled up on the floor of a stone cell.

There was a small, barred window, way high up, and she could sense that the bars were made of silver, would be impossible to break. A harsh ray of sunlight came through it on an angle, lighting up her face, and she squinted in pain. She rolled over, getting out of the way.

In the darkened corner, Caitlin breathed, slowly sitting up, trying to collect yourself. Her head was absolutely killing her, as she tried to remember.

She remembered being in a church. Santa Croce. She remembered being with Blake, ascending a pulpit. She remembered finding that secret compartment, opening it....

And then there had been a net thrown over her, her tackled to the ground. And then Kyle, looking down at her, his face grotesque. Kicking her.

She sat up straighter and looked around, feeling a throbbing bruise on her cheek. She was in a jail of some sort, probably put here by Kyle. She wondered how long she'd been here. Her throat was dry, and she felt weak. She listened, and in the distance, she heard what sounded like a faint cheer, followed by a massive vibration that shook the floor. She wondered where on earth she was.

She also wondered why she was alive. Why hadn't Kyle killed her? He was not one to show mercy. The only reason he would've kept her alive was if he planned on torturing her. Caitlin swallowed.

She wondered how she'd gotten into this mess to begin with. Everything was going so great, her idyllic time in Florence, her getting so close to finding her father, the clues all adding up. She had been so confident that she was almost there, right at the finish line.

Things had gone so wrong, so quickly. But how? She hadn't sensed Kyle's presence, or any of his people, at any point. He'd managed to sneak up on her so quickly. How had he found her? Had he been following her the whole time?

Caitlin wondered how that could be possible. The only person who knew she was there was Blake.

Blake.

Suddenly, her heart stopped. Had Blake led her to Kyle? Had he been deceiving her this whole time?

She felt her heart break at the thought. It hurt her more than anything she could imagine.

That *had* to be it. She'd been betrayed. She couldn't see what other possible explanation there could be. There was no other way Kyle could have found her. And what about Blake? She couldn't remember seeing him getting captured in the church. Granted, she couldn't see much as she was taken down so fast. But she didn't remember hearing him crying out, screaming.

And if Blake had been captured, wouldn't he be here, in the jail with her?

"Blake?" she called out.

She cleared her throat, rose to her feet, and screamed: "Blake!"

Her scream echoed again and again throughout the empty chambers, as if coming back to taunt her.

No answer. That settled it. He must have betrayed her.

She felt like such a fool for loving him. She felt so deceived, so betrayed. So stupid.

Caitlin suddenly heard the creaking of an iron door, followed by footsteps.

She stood on her feet, in the corner, and waited, prepared to fight for her life if need be.

She had a feeling, though, that it would be futile. Kyle was not a man to leave anything unplanned for. Knowing him, he probably had several backup plans to keep her locked down, tortured, or killed. Her chance of escape, she knew, would be almost none.

Kyle suddenly came into view. He appeared on the opposite side of the silver bars, faced her and grinned. It was more like a scowl.

Kyle had certainly seen better days. Half of his face was disfigured, and now he was missing an eye. He looked hideous, grotesque.

"How do you like your new accommodations?" he asked.

Caitlin said nothing, just stared back at him. Finally, she spit on the floor in his direction.

He laughed—an evil, creepy noise.

"You're right," he said. "Blake led us right to you. A lamb to slaughter. How could you have been so naïve? Well, finally, I have the upper hand. You have been a thorn in my side for as long as I can remember. It's thanks to you that my face is disfigured like this. That was my punishment for letting you go....Not this time."

Caitlin could feel the evil emanating off him, like a tangible thing. She had a sinking feeling that this might be the last moment of her life, and she prepared mentally to meet her fate.

"Before I kill you," Kyle continued, "I want you to know that I'm a very kind man. I'm going to offer you two options. To die quickly, easily and painlessly—or to die slowly, brutally. You still have a chance for the former, if you comply with what I have to say. If not, make no mistake about it: your fate will be beyond painful."

"I'm not afraid of dying slowly," Caitlin answered with contempt. "I'd rather die in one thousand hells than give you whatever you want."

Kyle smiled wider.

"You are a girl after my own heart," he said, licking his lips. "It's a shame that you and I never had a chance to be together. We would be a splendid couple."

She felt sick at the thought. "I had rather die," she answered.

He laughed out loud. "Don't worry, you will. Very soon. But before you do, I will make you this offer: give me the object that you found in the pulpit. We searched, and found nothing. Tell me what you did with it, where you managed to hide it before we caught you. Did you break it? Did you swallow it? What was it? Tell me, and I will spare you. In fact, if it's an answer I like, I might even let you go."

Caitlin thought, wracking her brain. She tried to remember, but her head was still foggy. What object was he talking about? What was it that he thought she'd found?

It started to slowly come back to her. What she'd found in the secret compartment. Kyle hadn't seen it, so of course he thought it was an object. What a fool.

What he didn't know, and what she would never tell him, was that there was no object at all. That it was a message. Inscribed in the stone. A message just for her: *the Rose and the Thorn meet in the Vatican.*

He would never understand what that meant. And she would never tell him.

Now, she was pleased. Let him think that there was a missing object.

"Yes," she lied, "I did find an object. And I destroyed it with my bare hands. Just like I would destroy you, if you were man enough to open these bars and give me the chance," she spat back, defiant.

At first, he scowled, but then he broke into a grin, wider and wider.

"You do not disappoint," he said. "Well, at least I tried. Now it's on to the good part. It's going to be fun watching you die slowly and painfully. In fact, I'm going to make sure that I have a front row seat."

Caitlin suddenly heard another cheer, this one louder, and felt the entire room shake. She wondered again what it could be, and where she was.

"You still have no idea where you are, do you?" he asked. "No, I can tell that you don't. You are one hundred feet beneath the earth, in the basement of the Roman Coliseum. Above us, the stadium is in use. By the grand vampire council. There are thousands of us up there, watching the games. Watching the brutal fights between vampire and human, between human and human, and between vampire and vampire. These fights offer us brutality beyond what we could ever hope to see elsewhere. It is one of our favorite spectator sports."

He got so close to the cell that she could smell his bad breath.

"And do you know who's going to be next in the show?" he asked.

He laughed aloud.

"Did you ever think you'd die here, of all places?"

Kyle turned to go, but before he did, he stopped and faced her.

"By the way," he said, "a present for you."

He threw something between the bars, and it landed on the floor of her cell.

Caitlin looked down at it: it looked like a small, silver necklace. It looked like *her* necklace.

"As the boy died, he called out for you. He seemed to really like you. Too bad you weren't there to protect him," Kyle said with a snort, then turned and stomped away.

Caitlin stopped breathing as she bent down and picked up the necklace. She looked closer, hoping beyond hoping that it wasn't really hers.

But it was. The one she had given to Jade.

There was no way that Kyle could possibly have this, unless it was true. Unless he had really killed Jade.

Caitlin felt a grief unlike any she'd ever known. She curled into a ball in the center of the floor, and broke down and sobbed. Her cries rose up, louder and louder, and mingled with the sound of the distant roar.

CHAPTER TWENTY SIX

Caitlin stood in silver shackles, before the entrance to the Coliseum. She'd been dragged there by two vampire guards, who'd shackled her in her cell by her hands and her feet, and led her up the stone stairs, down a ramp, and to this place. Now that she'd reached the upper levels, traveled down the ramp, and was really here, looking out, the view was awe-inspiring. And terrifying.

She had once gone to a baseball game, and she remembered the feeling of walking down the tunnel and first entering the bleachers, when the whole stadium opened up and thousands of eyes were upon her. This felt like that. But bigger. It was the biggest and most intimidating thing she had ever seen.

Before her was laid out the Roman coliseum, a massive arena, made entirely of stone. The stone was crumbling and deteriorated, and it had clearly been thousands of years since its heyday. But this vampire coven had somehow managed to bring it back to life. They didn't seem to care that they sat in crumbling bleachers. And they'd managed to cover up the crumbling floor with a floor of their own, turning this ancient relic into a functioning Coliseum once again.

Tens of thousands of malevolent vampire sat in the bleachers, looking down, cheering. Caitlin was surprised to see how deep the floor of the Coliseum actually went, sinking hundreds of feet beneath the earth, in a maze of tunnels and traps and compartments. The floor they put over it was covered in dirt and dust, which rose up in clouds in the sunlight. The two vampire guards prodded her forward, dragging her down the entranceway, and out onto the main floor.

A huge roar rose up, as Caitlin appeared out in the open. The sun beat down on her, and she squinted at the glare, trying to get her bearings.

The guards unlocked her shackles and gave her another hard shove, and she went flying into the stadium, rolling onto the ground.

Another roar erupted from the crowd.

Caitlin got to her feet and looked around, her eyes slowly adjusting to the bright light. She was standing alone, thousands of evil-looking vampires looking down at her, shaking their fists. She scanned the bleachers and saw, up high, in a special box, stood Kyle. Beside him stood the Grand Council, old, decrepit looking vampires in black robes and hoods.

The one in the center stepped forward and raised his hands, and the crowd quieted.

"My fellow vampires," he said, pausing dramatically. "Let the games begin!"

Another huge roar shook the Coliseum.

Caitlin heard a clang, then another, and looked down to see that the guards had thrown some weapons at her feet. She picked up a shield, a sword and a spear, which she shoved into her belt. She was dressed in a canvas tunic, crude and simple and rough against her skin.

She couldn't believe this was all happening. These sick vampires truly intended to kill her slowly. Somehow, they had managed to revive the cruel gladiator sport that people here had once enjoyed thousands of years ago. Weak, tired, confused, she felt a sense of despair, and wondered how she would ever survive.

Before Caitlin had a chance to take hold of her weapons, there came charging at her a dozen huge, muscle-bound warriors, all clad in full armor, all wielding fierce weaponry.

Caitlin could sense, as they approach, that they were humans. Still, they looked like formidable warriors, battle-scarred, and it looked like they had done this many times before. And survived.

They sprinted right for her, screaming with a battle cry, clearly wanting blood.

Caitlin focused, centered herself. She tried to remember all the things Aiden had taught her, all the techniques on Pollepel. She tried to breathe, to find the peace in the center of the storm.

She waited, a disciplined warrior. As they came within feet of her, she suddenly leapt into the air, way up high, did a somersault above their heads, and landed agilely behind them. She swung back around her as she did, and chopped off three of their heads.

The others kept running, falling into the dust, knocking each other over.

The crowd roared in surprise and delight.

The remaining warriors turned and faced her, indignant. They charged again.

This time, she stood and fought. She parried with them, blow for blow.

They were strong, and when one of their swords came down on her shield, she felt it reverberate throughout her entire body.

But she fought back valiantly. After all, she was quicker and faster than all of them. She was still a vampire.

Despite appearances, it was a mismatch. They were humans, and they fell like humans. Probably just a first attempt by the Grand

Council to warm her up, to see if she could handle the first wave of warriors. She got slashed and bruised, but nothing serious enough to bring her down.

Within minutes, the dozen warriors were but a heap of bodies around her.

She stood there, victorious, and the crowd quieted, then jumped to its feet and roared.

Even from here, Caitlin could see that Kyle and the Council were not pleased by this.

"Send in the Lions!" screamed the Council leader.

There came a roar of approval, and Caitlin hoped that it was not what it sounded like.

To her dread, it was. A side chamber opened in the Coliseum, and in raced ten lions, all charging right for her. They were huge, male lions, faster than she could have imagined, with long claws, and fangs bared. They gained speed with each passing step.

Caitlin reached down and extracted her short spear, and hurled it at the lead lion.

A direct hit between the eyes. He fell.

But the others didn't stop charging. She leapt high into the air just as one was about to pounce, leaping higher than the lion, and as she did, drove her short sword into its mane, behind his neck. Down it went.

She landed on the back of another line, reached under, and sliced its throat, and it went down with her.

Another lion pounced on her from behind, knocking her over, it's claws scraping up her back painfully.

On the ground, she wheeled, and sliced off its head with her sword.

The others pounced, too, but she was too quick for them. She suffered many scratches, and a nick from the fangs, but using her sword, she managed, after a long and gruesome fight, to bring the rest of them down.

Again, the crowd roared with approval.

She looked up and saw that Kyle and the judge were madder than ever. It looked like they had not expected her to make it this far.

The Council leader turned to Kyle, and he nodded back gravely. The judge then held out his thumb, and turned it down.

As he did, a huge metal door opened, and out came a single warrior.

He was clad in all black armor, with a black helmet, holding a sword and a shield.

Caitlin could sense, even from this distance, that he was not human. It was a vampire, and a formidable one. This frightened her more than all the rest.

Moreover, she could already sense that this was no ordinary vampire. It was someone she knew. Even from here, she could sense it.

And then, she realized: it was Blake.

Blake.

He lifted back his helmet, and stared at her. Caitlin's heart wrenched with grief at the sight.

So, she realized. It was true. He had deceived her after all.

Blake shook his head.

"Caitlin!" he yelled out. "I did not betray you. They captured me, too. I promise you. I did not lead them to you."

"Then why do you stand there, ready to fight me?" Caitlin called back.

"I've been forced into this stadium," he yelled back. "But I will not fight you. As I told them before."

Blake walked out to the center of the stadium, faced Kyle and the judges, and threw down his shield, helmet, and sword.

"I will NOT fight her!" he screamed back at them.

The crowd booed in disapproval.

Caitlin was shocked at this turn of events. Was it just another trick? Was he just waiting to deceive her again? Or had she been wrong all along about him? Had he been faithful to her all this time? Now, she was not so sure.

The judge stood. "If you do not fight her, you will suffer in unimaginable death!" he yelled back. "Choose!"

"Kill me as you will," he yelled back. "I shall never fight her!"

The crowd booed again, and the judge nodded at the guards.

Suddenly, Caitlin felt herself being shackled from behind by several guards, the silver shackles rendering her helpless as she was dragged off the stadium floor. She dug her heels in, trying to resist, but it was no use. They dragged her into a holding pen, off to the side.

She watched Blake, standing there, defiant. And in that moment, she realized. It was not a trick. He had never betrayed her. Not only that, but he was preparing to sacrifice his own life for hers.

Even worse, she had gotten him into this mess: if he had not come with her on her mission, he would be back safe at home right now. She felt worse than ever. And she felt so mad at herself for jumping to conclusions, for assuming the worst. Why couldn't she have given him the benefit of the doubt?

As Caitlin stood chained in the pen, helpless, she suddenly saw a side door of the Coliseum open, and two dozen of the most vicious looking vampires she had ever seen charge out, on horseback, for Blake.

Blake wheeled and hurried to grab his sword and shield.

He faced them down as they charged, prepared to make a stand.

They came at him in full force, slashing at him, and he fought back bravely, knocking several off their horses. Soon, they were mostly on foot, coming at him from every direction, and he fought like the skilled warrior he was. He killed two of them in a single blow.

But he was outnumbered. As Caitlin watched, her heart breaking, she saw that he was getting weaker, slashed in several directions. He was not going to win.

Caitlin felt the injustice of it all, and suddenly felt the rage overcome her. A hot flash raised up, from her toes up through her body, and she felt herself infused with a superhuman strength. She willed herself to be stronger than she had ever been, and in one strong motion, she reached back, and with all her might, snapped her chains.

She leapt over the wall, grabbed her weapons, and sprinted for Blake

The crowd roared in approval, jumping to its feet.

Caitlin charged at the group of vampires encircling him. One vampire, on his horse, was about to stab Blake from behind, and Caitlin took aim and threw her spear at him; it went right through the back of his neck, and he fell off his horse, dead.

The crowd roared.

She grabbed the fallen vampire's sword, leapt onto his horse, and charged at the others, swinging as she went.

The rage built and built, and Caitlin felt a primordial strength that she never had. She charged and swung and struck and jabbed, and she was a whirlwind of destruction.

Within minutes, she managed to kill several of the vampires around Blake.

She dismounted and stood at his side.

The two of them stood there, back to back, fighting, only a few vampires remaining.

Blake, emboldened, managed to kill the vampire facing him, while Caitlin killed one more, and focused on the other two.

She attacked one, stabbing him in the heart, but as she did, she left herself carelessly open to attack. The other vampire lunged at her open back, his sword aiming right for her kidney, and Caitlin saw it coming. But she couldn't react in time. She knew that it was too late, and that she would certainly die.

She braced herself for the horrible pain—but to her surprise, it didn't come. Instead, she heard a horrible scream, and she looked over to see Blake standing there, to see that he had stepped in the way, and had taken the blow for her. The vampire had stabbed him, instead, right through the heart.

Caitlin stepped up and chopped off the vampire's head. As she did, her bracelet, the one Blake had bought her, fell off her wrist, to the ground.

At the same time, the vampire fell to the ground, the last of them, dead.

Blake sank to his knees, dying.

As he collapsed to the ground, Caitlin caught him, let him gently down. She reached up and tried to remove the sword from his heart, but he grunted out in pain, and she knew to let it be.

She cradled his head in her hands, and knelt over him, crying.

"I want you to know," he said with effort, blood dripping from his mouth, "that I never betrayed you."

"I know," Caitlin said through tears. "Blake, I'm so sorry."

He nodded, then smiled at her weakly, blood on his lips.

"I love you," he said. "And I always will."

He put his hand into hers, thrusting something into her palm, and then closed his eyes, dead.

She looked down, and saw that it was a piece of sea glass. The piece from Pollepel.

Caitlin leaned back and wailed, a horrible wail of grief. She had never felt so torn apart. She would have given anything for that sword to have struck her instead.

The crowd, at first shocked, now erupted into a roar of approval.

"CAITLIN! CAITLIN!" they chanted. Their screams and stamping shook the entire stadium.

It was clearly not the reaction that Kyle and the judges had hoped for.

They both got up and stormed away from their balcony, shutting down the games for the day.

CHAPTER TWENTY SEVEN

Caitlin ran. She was in a field of flowers, up to her waist, the flowers a brilliant medley of colors. It was a bright day, the sun directly overhead, and in the distance, her father waited.

But as she ran, the flowers turned into a field of swords, all plunged into the earth, their tips sticking up and shaking in the wind. She ran through them, cutting a path, heading for her father.

This time, there was nothing between the two of them. As she ran and ran, he got closer. She ran for all she had, and soon, she was in his arms.

She could not believe it, but she was really in his arms.

He hugged her, and she could feel his strength coursing through her body. It was the hug of a father who loved her, the father she'd always longed to have. She wanted to crane back her head, to look up at his face, but she was too happy to just be in his arms.

"I'm so proud of you," he said over her shoulder. "You are your father's daughter."

She smiled, feeling totally encased in warmth.

"When will I see you?" she asked.

"Tomorrow," he said, firmly.

He pulled her back, and looked down at her intently. The fierceness of his eyes burned through her. They were like two burning suns, staring right at her, and she almost had to look away from the intensity of it.

"Tomorrow. We will be together, forever."

Caitlin sat upright, breathing hard.

She looked all about herself, and realized that it was just a dream. She was back in her cell.

It had felt so real, felt as if her father had been with her, right there in the room. As she rubbed her arms and shoulders, she could still feel his warmth.

What had the dream meant? It was so different than the others. She had never had one like it before.

She would see him tomorrow. Did that mean that this would be her last day on earth? That she would be crossing over to the other side, seeing him in heaven?

She thought back to the day before, to the fierce fighting. She stood and stretched her limbs slowly, and felt an ache in all of them. She was covered with cuts and scratches and bruises, wounds which, for a vampire, should have healed more quickly. But these were deep wounds: sword slashes, buckler punctures, lion bites. She was rusty. It ached for her just to walk across the room. She had no idea how she could survive another day of fighting.

More than anything, she pained to think of Blake. She remembered his last gruesome moments, as he was killed by those vampires. His dying in her arms. His final words. She felt like dying herself.

She had been so wrong about him. She should have run to his defense sooner. She blamed herself. And she wished the sword blow had been for her.

Caitlin looked up, as several vampire guards suddenly appeared, the silver shackles at the ready. They opened her silver cell door, and she knew that within a matter of moments, she would be back out there for round two.

She thought of her father, of how they would be together soon. At least, that was some solace. Perhaps, soon, this would all be over.

*

Standing at the entrance tunnel, Caitlin was unshackled by the guards, and she walked freely out into the Coliseum's floor. She needed no prodding this time. She was eager to meet the day, to fight again, to finally meet her destiny. She was tired, deeply tired. Everyone she had loved, she had lost. Sam. Caleb. Blake. Her father. Rose. Jade….There seemed to be no end to the loss.

She was tired of trying to hold onto everything. If today was going to be her last day—and she felt that it was—then she was prepared. She would go down in style. She would give all these ghoulish vampires the spectacle they wanted, and fight with more ferocity than she'd ever had.

As she walked out onto the Coliseum, thousands of vampires rose their feet, chanting her name: "CAITLIN! CAITLIN!"

Caitlin looked up and saw the judge stand in his booth, Kyle at his side. They both scowled down at her.

"And now," yelled the judge, "the elephants!"

A huge roar rose up. On the far side of the Coliseum, an enormous door opened.

Caitlin couldn't believe it. Charging right at her, single file, was a herd of elephants. She counted six of them. The ground shook with each step they took.

They raised back their heads and roared. The roar alone nearly split her ears.

The crowd, thrilled, cheered them on.

On top of each elephant rode a vicious vampire. These vampires were different—bigger than the others, covered in a slick black armor from head to toe, with grotesque masks covering their faces. They carried long swords, javelins, crossbows, and all sort of weaponry.

Caitlin looked down at her puny sword and shield, and realized she was terribly outmatched. It wouldn't even be a fair battle.

She closed her eyes and breathed deep. She tried to enter another realm, to enter a state where fighting meant not fighting. She tried to remember everything that Aiden taught her.

When you are outmatched by strength, do not resist. Use your opponent's strength against him.

Caitlin tried to block out all the noise, all the action around her. She forced herself to focus on the closest elephant, charging right for her.

The vampire riding it leaned back and aimed his spear at her.

She pretended not to notice, as moments later, he hurled it.

At the last second, she rolled out of the way, let the spear plunge into the ground beside her.

It was a close call, and the crowd gasped in disappointment.

She rolled over, extracted the spear from the ground, and knelt down low. The elephant was only feet away, and as it lifted its huge foot, about to stomp her, Caitlin lodged the base of the spear into the ground, its tip pointing up, and got out of the way.

The horrific screech of the elephant filled the air, as it stepped down on the spear tip. The screech shook the entire stadium, as the spear lodged its way into the elephant's foot.

The elephant collapsed to its knees with a tremendous crash, and its rider went flying off, headfirst into the ground. As the animal collapsed, belly first, it crushed its rider beneath it.

The other elephants, right behind it, couldn't stop in time. They all tripped over their compatriot, and they all went crashing to the ground, rolling every which way. All of their riders went flying off.

The crowd roared.

Caitlin took advantage of the chaos. She grabbed a spear and threw it, piercing one vampire right through the neck.

She bounded on top of another elephant, ripped the sword from its disoriented owner's hand, and decapitated him.

She leapt from elephant to elephant, tracking down each vampire, attacking with the sword.

In moments, she had killed nearly all of them, all too shaken to react on time.

Except for one, and he managed to dodge her strike. He spun around, and cracked her hard in the back of the head with his shield.

She felt the pain in her head as she fell to her face.

He jabbed his spear right for her throat, but she rolled out of the way just in time.

She leaned back and kicked him hard, right in the groin, and as he knelt down, she spun to the side and kicked him hard across the face. He went down.

She jumped to her feet, raised her sword, and before he could get up again, she decapitated him.

The stunned stadium was completely silent for a moment.

Then, suddenly, as one, they all jumped to their feet, roaring her name.

The judge, outraged, leapt to his feet.

"BRING IN THE GIANT!" he yelled.

Before Caitlin could catch her breath, another side compartment opened, and in rushed a massive giant.

The crowd roared.

Caitlin's eyes opened wide in disbelief. She had never seen a monster like this. This creature was at least one hundred feet tall, and, like a

Cyclops, had just one eye, in the center of its head. She didn't imagine that such things even walked the earth, and she could see its muscles rippling out in every direction.

It leaned back its head and roared, and the Coliseum shook; if possible, it was even louder than the roar of the elephants.

Caitlin swallowed. She had no idea how to fight a creature like this.

Before she could even react, the giant, surprising her with its speed, took a huge step towards her, swiped his hand down and swatted her.

Caitlin was thrown across the Stadium, hundreds of feet, slamming into a wall, and felt the wind knocked out of her.

The crowd roared.

Caitlin was on the ground, her head killing her, trying to catch her breath. She was still in shock that something that big could move that fast.

The giant swung again, bringing his fist down to crush her.

She rolled out of the way just in time, and the blow left a huge hole in the earth, where the giant's hand got lodged.

Caitlin rolled over, grabbed her sword, and in one quick move, brought it down hard on the giant's wrist, before he could extract his fist.

It worked: she managed to chop off his hand.

The giant leaned back and screeched, blood squirting like a river from his arm, all over her, all over the vampire audience. Instead of being horrified by it, the vampires seemed to relish it, even tried to lap up the blood as it landed on them.

The giant, in a fury, chased after Caitlin with a vengeance. But it was too clouded by anger. It couldn't think straight. It swept at her wildly with its free hand, missing each time. Caitlin ran and ran, trying to make it to the long javelin she saw in the distance.

Finally, she made it. She grabbed it, rolled hard, just missing the giant's swipe, and then leaned back and hurled it with all she had, aiming right for the giant's eye.

A direct hit. The long javelin went through the giant's eye, and out the other side.

For a second, the giant froze. Then like an enormous tree, it fell sideways. It crashed to the ground, shaking the Coliseum so hard that it knocked the vampires out of their seats.

The crowd went crazy. It jumped to its feet, roaring and roaring.

"She has won clemency!" the crowd members screamed. "Let her free. Let her free!"

A huge chorus of approval ripped through the stadium.

But the judge did not give in. Instead, he looked at Kyle, who nodded back, and then he stood. The crowd quieted.

"Bring in our last warrior!" he yelled.

Caitlin was so tired, so out of breath, so disoriented. She couldn't imagine what else they had to throw at her. She felt confident that, whatever it was, she would not have the energy left to face it.

The doors opened, and out came a single warrior, a man about her size, about her height, looking a lot like her. He wore dark, fitted armor, and held a gleaming sword and shield.

His helmet up, she could clearly see his face.

It was the one warrior she knew she could never kill.

Facing her, was her brother Sam.

CHAPTER TWENTY EIGHT

Caitlin's heart whirled with emotions.

Sam. Her little brother. Here. Back in time. In Rome. In the Coliseum of all places. On the one hand, she was thrilled to see him.

On the other, he stood there, in battle gear, facing her down, a weapon in hand. And with a look on his face meant to kill. How could this be?

How had it come to this? What had they done to him?

She could sense, even from this great distance, that he was a vampire. She tried to sense his feelings towards her, but it was obscured. As if he were deliberately blocking them.

More than anything, she felt sad. Betrayed. Confused. Was it not enough that he'd had to ruin things for her in the 21st century? Had he had to come back now, and still make things hard for her?

And after all that she had done for him. All through his life, she had always looked out for him, always been the one he could turn to. She'd always tried to help him, to save him.

Had it really come to this? Did he really hate his own sister enough to kill her? Or was he just still dazed? Under the influence of this evil coven's spell?

"Sam!" she yelled out. "It's me! Caitlin. Your sister!"

She hoped that by vocalizing it, he would come to himself, would recognize her, snap out of it, lay down his weapons.

"I don't want to fight you!" she yelled. "I don't want to hurt you!"

The crowd booed.

Sam walked out towards the center, closer and closer to her. But instead of dropping his weapons, as she'd hoped, he lowered his face mask with a definitive clang, and raised his sword and shield.

The crowd roared in approval. Even Kyle smiled down.

Caitlin's heart pounded. She really didn't want to hurt her little brother.

Before she could think, before she could decide what to do, she found herself being charged by Sam.

He swung his sword down at her with a ferocious speed, and Caitlin barely managed to duck out of the way.

The crowd roared.

"Sam!" she cried, desperate, and afraid. She was afraid he would hurt her—but even more, afraid she might be forced to hurt him. "Listen to me! Please!"

But he swung at her again, and she leaned back and barely missed the below. He was faster than she had thought, and extremely powerful.

As he came at her with a flurry of blows, she raised her shield. She blocked them, but she felt herself getting pushed back, further and further. She couldn't bring herself to swing back. But his blows were so unexpected, so strong, they threw her completely off balance.

She stumbled and fell to the ground, and the crowd roared, on its feet, tasting blood.

"KILL HER!" the crowd roared, on its feet.

"Bring me the spear!" Sam yelled.

Caitlin was shocked at her little brother's voice. It was so deep, so dark. It was the voice of a man.

Kyle, high up, nodded down to an attendant, and he came running out and handed Sam a huge, golden spear.

Caitlin used the time to scurry back to her feet, to backup, to consider all her options.

What could she possibly do? Kill her own brother?

No. She could not. She was tired of fighting. And if even her own brother wanted to kill her, then what was the point in living anymore?

She stared at him, hoping one last time that he would come to, that he would see it was his sister.

And then she dropped her sword. And her shield. And closed her eyes.

She stood there, defenseless, wide open, an easy target.

Sam faced her, and slowly lifted the heavy, golden spear.

"KILL HER! KILL HER!" chanted the crowd.

Caitlin opened her eyes.

In that moment, she felt the whole world in slow motion. She saw every last detail, heard every little sound, as the rest of the world was slowly muted out. She felt the breeze on her skin, noticed the brilliance of the sun. She felt strongly that this would be her last moment on Earth.

And she looked forward to it, to finally seeing her father. What a fitting way to see him, she thought. Sent by his own son's hand.

Sam took a step forward, reached back, and suddenly, he hurled the spear.

As Caitlin opened her eyes, she was shocked by what she saw.

At the last second, Sam had turned on his heel, and hurled the spear not at her—but rather, had aimed it up, at the bleachers.

Directly at Kyle.

It all happened so fast, was so unexpected, that Kyle had no time to react.

Before he could get out of the way, the spear went through his arm, and kept going, through the judge's heart. The two of them shrieked, stuck together.

The entire crowd jumped to its feet, in shock and outrage.

"Kill them!" Kyle screamed.

But before anyone could react, the sky suddenly turned black.

Flying over the Coliseum, there suddenly descended hundreds of vampires.

Caitlin didn't need to look up to know who it was.

There, up in the sky, leading them, was Caleb. By his side was Samuel, Aiden, Polly, and hundreds of others.

Caleb wasted no time. He dove right for Kyle, grabbing him by the throat, wrestling him down to the bleachers.

The hundreds of other vampires descended, too, prepared for battle against the thousands. It was all-out war, hand to hand.

Sam came running over to Caitlin, tearing off his helmet.

"I hope you understand," he said. "I had to trick them. To catch them off guard. I never meant to hurt you. It was the only way," he said. "I'm here, I'm back in time, because I love you. And because I'm sorry."

They embraced.

But they had no time to waste. Thousands of vampires were pouring out of the bleachers, charging for them.

Sam turned to her. "Can you still fly?"

She nodded, and they both took off into the air, flying, rising high above the din of vampires sprinting for them.

As they flew over the bleachers, they passed Kyle, wrestling with Caleb.

Caleb had the upper hand, but for a moment, he slipped; Kyle took advantage, grabbed his sword, and reached back to stab Caleb.

Sam and Caitlin dove low. Just in time, she kicked the sword out of Kyle's hand; Sam, right behind her, then kicked Kyle hard in the face, sending him flying head over heels over the balcony.

Caitlin reached down and grabbed Caleb.

"Are you okay?"

He looked at her.

"Caitlin," he said, his eyes brimming over. "I know now. I know who you are. I remember everything," he hugged her tight. "And I'm so sorry."

She felt her whole world warm up inside her, as she hugged him back.

She pulled him back and looked at him with intensity.

"I know where it is," she said quickly to Caleb. "The Shield."

Sam and Caleb both crowded close, anxious to hear, their eyes opened wide.

"Follow me," she said.

CHAPTER TWENTY NINE

Caitlin, Caleb, and Sam flew over Rome, racing to bridge the short distance from the Coliseum to the Vatican. Caitlin had never been to the Vatican before, and she followed Caleb's lead. She'd been worried for a moment that Caleb wouldn't come at all. Back there, in the Coliseum, he didn't want to leave; he'd been set on diving down and finding Kyle in the crowd, on exacting revenge for Jade. But Caitlin had begged to him let it go for another time. She argued that he would endanger them all by getting bogged down in a fight with those thousands of vampires, and that they'd never accomplish what was more important for the race: finding the Shield. Finally, reluctantly, he'd conceded.

As they rounded a bend, Vatican City came into view, and Caitlin was shocked. She had somehow expected the Vatican to be a single building, and was surprised to see that it was in fact an entire city. From this bird's eye view, she could see building after building, dominated by the huge, dome of St. Peter's Chapel. She was breathless at its magnitude.

"We'll have to land at the main entrance," Caleb said. "The Vatican is heavily guarded by our kind. There's no way in or out without permission. It's the oldest and most powerful vampire coven there is. No one has ever tried to attack them, not even Kyle's people, and no one probably ever will. They stand guard over vampire relics and secrets unlike any the world has ever known.

"They also have weapons unlike any the world has ever seen. If we arrive at their doors, and they don't grant us permission, they may very well kill us on the spot. Knocking on their door is not something one does lightly. The only way they'll let us in is if they perceive you to be one of their own, one of their coven. That will depend on who your father was. Let's hope."

Caitlin sensed a presence behind her, and as she turned, saw, on the horizon, a swarm of black. Hundreds of vampires of the Grand Council were following them. Caitlin saw Kyle at their head, arm bleeding, and scowling with fury.

"Looks like we have company," she said.

Caleb and Sam turned, and frowned.

"No time to waste," Caleb said.

The three of them took a sharp dive, right down to the entrance of the Vatican.

They ran up to its huge, main doors, and they suddenly opened. Out came a short, old man, wearing a white cloak and hood.

He pulled back his hood to reveal glowing, light green eyes. He stared at the three of them, then took a step towards Caitlin.

"You've arrived," he said to her.

It was clear that he had been expecting her. The three of them exchanged a look of relief.

He turned and they followed him inside, and he shut the door behind them.

Seconds later, they heard a loud crashing at the door, as the hundreds of other vampires tried to get in.

Caitlin, Caleb and Sam wheeled, ready to fight.

"Do not worry," the man said calmly. "Regular vampires are defenseless against this building."

Caitlin looked up, and saw other vampires trying to fly over the wall, to dive down. But as they did, they bounced back, as if hitting an invisible shield.

"It is protected. Only the holy can enter."

They walked quickly down the corridor, passing a beautiful open grass courtyard, with a fountain in its center. It felt very much like a cloister inside, as they passed rows and rows of arched stone walls.

They followed the man into another building, and down an endlessly long corridor. The ceiling was high and arched, covered in brightly painted frescoes.

They walked and walked, at a fast pace. It felt like they were walking forever, until finally they turned down yet another corridor, climbed a set of stairs, and entered the most magnificent room Caitlin had ever seen.

She looked up, awestruck.

"The Sistine Chapel," Caleb whispered.

The three of them entered the huge room, and she could not look away from Michelangelo's ceiling. Every inch of it, spanning hundreds of feet, was covered in brightly-painted scenes. It was so vibrant, so life-like, it felt like a living thing.

Caitlin heard a shuffling, and looked over and saw hundreds of vampires in the room, all dressed in white, wearing white hoods, and lined up patiently along the walls.

In the center of the room, on a raised dais, stood an altar, and before that stood three more vampires. Their dress was more elaborate than the others, in white robes with gold trim.

The vampire that led them in gestured for the three of them to approach the altar.

Caitlin walked slowly up the dais and before the three vampires, accompanied by Caleb and Sam. Her heart was pounding. Was her father among these men? What was this coven, exactly? She felt closer to her father than she'd ever had. Felt as if he were in this very room with her.

The vampire in the center slowly pulled back his hood and stared at her with his huge, glowing, light blue eyes. His eyes were so large, so translucent, it felt as if he were not of this Earth.

"We are members of the most holy and most ancient and most powerful vampire coven ever known to man. We have lived thousands of years longer than anyone else, and we guard secrets that no one else is fit to protect. It is thanks to us that the human and vampire races have managed to survive. Few know of our existence—and even fewer are members. Your father is one of us. Which means that you, too, are one of us."

Caitlin's heart pounded in her chest. The implications of it seemed overwhelming. These were her father's people. Here, in the Vatican. She felt so proud of him, and felt special herself. Yet she also burned with questions.

He suddenly held out a small, jewel-encrusted box.

"Your key, please," he said.

Caitlin looked back at him, puzzled.

Key?

She didn't have a key. Had they mistaken her for someone else?

He looked down and pointed at her necklace.

Caitlin reached down and felt it, forgetting it was even there. Her necklace.

She removed it, stepped forward, and slowly inserted it into the small keyhole.

She turned, and to her surprise, it opened softly.

Inside it, was another key, large and gold.

"Take it," he said. "It belongs to you."

Caitlin reached in and took the key, her mind racing. It was heavy, smooth. She could feel an incredible power coming off of it.

"It is one of the four keys," the man said. "Only you can find the other three. When you have all four, you will meet your father. And he will give you the Shield.

"You are on a very sacred mission," he added. "You must find him. For all of us."

"But where is he?" she asked.

"He does not live in this time," he answered. "You will have to go back, further."

Caitlin's mind spun. *Go back in time? Again?*

The vampire nodded, and the hundreds of vampires in the room came forward and crowded around them, in a tight circle.

The three vampires stepped forward, and each held out a jewel-encrusted chalice, filled with a white liquid.

"White blood," he said. "The holiest of bloods. You must each take three sips."

Caitlin, Caleb, and Sam each took a chalice.

Caitlin drank, taking three sips, wondering what would happen. She was surprised by how sweet it was.

More and more vampires crowded around them, closer and closer. They all lowered their heads, as if in prayer, and began to chant.

"…to resurrect another day," they finished chanting, "in God's ultimate grace."

No, Caitlin thought.

She began to feel light-headed. This can't be happening. Not so soon. There was so many questions she had left to ask. Who were these people? How long had they lived? How had they know her father? What was he like? What was the next step on her mission? What time and place where they sending her to?

And there were so many questions she needed to ask Caleb. How much did he really remember? Would he go back with her, together, this time? Would he remember?

323

And most of all, did he still love her? Would he love her again? Would they have another child?

She needed some time to prepare for the transition. Even just a few minutes.

But it was not meant to be.

As the vampires continued with the funeral service, repeating it a second time, she felt increasingly light-headed.

She grabbed Caleb's hand tightly, and she felt him grab hers back. It felt so good to be with him, to be by his side. She hoped it would never end. She hoped that this time they would go back together, never leave each other's sides. She never wanted to be apart from him again.

As they began the funeral service a third time, she felt him lean over and whisper, "I love you, Caitlin. And I always will."

She felt herself getting lighter and lighter, drifting towards the ceiling, towards the sky, towards some far-off place where heaven and earth met.

And she knew, she just *knew*, that there was something bigger than this world. That there was some magical opening in the universe where destiny and love prevailed. And that, no matter what, she and Caleb would be together again.

COMING SOON...

Book #5 in the Vampire Journals

Please visit Morgan's site, where you can join the mailing list, hear the latest news, see additional images, and find links to stay in touch with Morgan on Facebook, Twitter, Goodreads and elsewhere:

www.morganricebooks.com

Also by Morgan Rice

turned
(book #1 in the Vampire Journals)

loved
(Book #2 in the Vampire Journals)

betrayed
(Book #3 in the Vampire Journals)

CPSIA information can be obtained at www.ICGtesting.com
Printed in the USA
BVOW04s1354190913

331495BV00001B/6/P